By Lynn Cahoon

The Tuesday Night Survivors' Club

The Tourist Trap Mysteries
Wedding Bell Blues
Picture Perfect Frame
Murder in Waiting
Memories and Murder
Killer Party
Hospitality and Homicide
Tea Cups and Carnage
Murder on Wheels
Killer Run
Dressed to Kill
If the Shoe Kills
Mission to Murder
Guidebook to Murder
Novellas
A Very Mummy Holiday
Mother's Day Mayhem
Corned Beef and Casualties
Santa Puppy
A Deadly Brew
Rockets' Dead Glare

The Kitchen Witch Mysteries
One Poison Pie
Two Wicked Desserts
Three Tainted Teas

Novellas
Chili Cauldron Curse
Murder 101
Have a Holly, Haunted Christmas

The Tuesday Night Survivors' Club

A Survivors' Book Club Mystery

Lynn Cahoon

LYRICAL UNDERGROUND
Kensington Publishing Corp.
www.kensingtonbooks.com

LYRICAL PRESS BOOKS are published by

Kensington Publishing Corp.
119 West 40th Street
New York, NY 10018

All Kensington titles, imprints, and distributed lines are available at special quantity discounts for bulk purchases for sales promotion, premiums, fund-raising, educational, or institutional use.

Special book excerpts or customized printings can also be created to fit specific needs. For details, write or phone the office of the Kensington Sales Manager: Kensington Publishing Corp., 119 West 40th Street, New York, NY 10018. Attn. Sales Department. Phone: 1-800-221-2647.

Lyrical Press and Lyrical Press logo Reg. U.S. Pat. & TM Off.

First Electronic Edition: June 2022
ISBN: 978-1-5161-1113-8 (ebook)

First Print Edition: June 2022
ISBN: 978-1-5161-1114-5

Printed in the United States of America

To the nurse who taught me that I was enjoying reading cozy mysteries during my cancer treatment. Your bag of books that Sunday morning made all the difference.

ACKNOWLEDGMENTS

Although this book/series is set in Sedona, and I used several real local tourist stops in the book, the story, characters, and settings (like the Next Chapter Bookstore) are my own creation and fictional. There are a ton of people who were in my life during my cancer journey that added to this story. Know that you made my life a little less crazy those days—including my own alpha hero who shaved his head the Sunday afternoon when I started losing my hair due to the chemo treatments. As far as writing this book, thank you to Esi Sogah and the Kensington team for picking the series out of the list of possible ideas. And as always, thanks to my agent, Jill Marsal.

Chapter 1

Rarity Cole was living and loving her second shot at life. If she'd been a cat, she would have eight left. Right now, she was just grateful to have this second chance after living through the breast cancer that had been almost too advanced. Now, in the bookstore she'd cashed in her corporate stocks to buy, she felt at home. She shelved the last book from the box that had arrived this morning into her new healing section. It still looked a little sparse, but she was determined to give others like her options when the *C* word was thrown around by the team of doctors who seemed to think they had total control over you and your body.

Which reminded her, she still needed to find an oncologist in the area. The doctors from St. Louis had pressed how important it was to keep on the medical regimen they'd started her on, which meant not only taking a pill every day, but getting regular blood work and mammograms to make sure she was okay. She'd spent long enough pretending she wasn't still recovering from the cancer treatments. It was time to check into her body again. She took the empty box back to the main counter and wrote the task on the to-do list that she kept on the counter.

The air-conditioning blowing out of the nearby vent made her shiver, and she rubbed her arms before finding a sweater to put on. If she turned it down, she started to sweat every time someone opened the door to The Next Chapter, her new bookstore in downtown Sedona, Arizona. Her shop was positioned right between a fortune teller's shop and a place that sold crystals. The crystal shop was owned by Rarity's best friend from high school, Sam Aarons. Sam was the one who had talked her into moving here and away from St. Louis a few months ago.

Honestly, she didn't mind the new location. It was in keeping with the new her. When you rang the bell at the oncologist's office, you tended to reevaluate your life. Gratitude for what you gained and what you currently have.

Which was, in Rarity's case, a few extra pounds around the middle and a need for a nap at least once a day. Eating right and exercise hadn't stopped the ten-pound weight gain that had circled her waist. And stuck.

Rarity blamed the chocolate. She'd eaten a lot of chocolate, and ice cream and fast food during her year of treatment. Then the visits had just stopped. She had seen her doctor once since she'd been "cured" and once before she'd left St. Louis. They'd drawn blood to check to see if the cancer had returned. Or worse, if the treatment was now killing her instead of the disease. Doctor visits were always a barrel of fun.

The bell over the door sounded, and she watched someone walk toward the counter.

"I'm here for the meeting tonight?" A fiftyish woman stood in front of the counter. "I know I'm early, but I was so excited when I read about your new book club in the Sunday paper. I'm Shirley Prescott. I rang the bell after completing treatments two years ago. Although, I'm still going to my oncologist every six months. They call it a well-baby checkup. And I'm rambling. George always says I ramble, and since having cancer, I'm worse. I guess I want to get out all my words before something else happens because tomorrow's not promised."

Rarity took an instant liking to the woman. Shirley's chattering was refreshing after hanging out in a quiet bookstore and then going home to an empty house. "I'm Rarity Cole, owner of The Next Chapter, and I'll be leading the group tonight. I'm almost at a year. Survivor. I always hated that term. But you work with what you're given, right?"

"I feel like I should have done something heroic to be called a survivor. Like survived a month in the desert or walked away from a plane crash. I just went to every appointment and did what they told me. Well, except for losing weight. I started baking again, and George doesn't eat sweets. So there's that." Shirley glanced around at the area by the fireplace. "I see you found Annie's Bakery. She bakes the best cookies in town. Well, besides me."

"Go grab a drink and a few cookies." Rarity looked at the clock. It was almost seven, and Shirley looked like the only participant in the book club. Rarity had needed books when she went through treatment, but maybe having a group called the survivors' book club was off-putting. Like what Shirley said. "We'll get started in a few minutes."

Shirley handed her a piece of paper. "Before I forget, George wanted to know if you could order these books for him. They're all on World War I or maybe II. I forget what he's currently researching. He makes planes and boats and stuff. You should see our basement, it's filled with his models."

"Sounds like a fun hobby." She glanced at the list. "I don't think I have any of these in stock, but I can have them for next week's meeting. I'll just need a credit card to charge them on."

Shirley dug in her tote and pulled out a wallet. She handed over a card. "Set me up a tab because I'm going to be your best customer. George hates driving into Flagstaff to get supplies. And when I was going through treatment, he'd complain for a week after I had chemo about how long the drive was."

"I bet you were glad for the company." Rarity thought about how Kevin hadn't come once to her treatments, saying that hospitals made him sick.

"Yeah, as much as he griped, he'd bring games and cards. We had fun." Shirley smiled at the memory. "Which I know sounds totally weird. Anyway, I'll go get settled. You do what you need to do, don't worry about me."

It was already ten after seven, so Rarity ordered George's books, set up a contact file for Shirley and George, and then took the credit card back to where Shirley was sitting. She had taken out a pile of pink yarn and a crochet hook and had started working on the project in her lap. Rarity held out the card. "Here you go. That's pretty."

"It's for my granddaughter. Karen and her husband are expecting. I've been working on this off and on for a month. I need to get it done, but it's so hot. Sometimes I wish we still lived in Idaho. Getting through the winters there, I needed a project on my lap." Shirley tucked the card into her wallet. "I'm sorry we didn't get more of a crowd. I'll bring someone next week. I promise. I hope you're not thinking of cancelling the club."

"No, there's no need to cancel. It takes time to build a group." Rarity sat next to the pile of books she'd chosen for possible discussions. "Have you read any of these?"

Shirley shook her head. "During treatment I didn't read anything but cozy mysteries. I could lose myself in the plot or the setting. I'm looking forward to expanding my reading choices."

Rarity moved the cozy mysteries she'd pulled into a side pile. "Okay then, I'll take these off the list."

"Maybe someone else will want to read those," Shirley protested.

Rarity glanced around at the empty chairs. "I don't hear anyone complaining. Let's look at the women's fiction. I wanted to start with a book that didn't talk about cancer, but instead dealt with a woman struggling with other problems."

They discussed the books until there were only five left on the table. Rarity heard the clock chime eight thirty. "We did a lot of work tonight."

"We didn't even choose a book." Shirley pointed to the table. "We still have five up for contention."

"We can make the decision next week. I'll put these on the counter with a flyer about how we're going to choose one to read next week. Maybe that will draw some more people into the group." Rarity could already see the flyer in her mind. She'd make it first thing in the morning.

"You're really good at this marketing thing." Shirley tucked her blanket into her tote bag. "I'm happy you moved here and opened your shop. I've missed being part of a book club."

"I'm glad I did as well." She glanced around at the old building with high ceilings with tin plating on them. She didn't know what the utility costs would be to keep this place cool, but she loved the look of the old brick and the warm wood floors. "It's beginning to feel like home."

* * * *

Wednesday morning, Rarity made the book club sign and display and then went about what was becoming her normal routine. She'd worked as a business analyst at a large corporation before leaving St. Louis, and she'd thought her days were busy then. She had quickly found out that owning the bookstore meant no day was the same. She needed to start setting up some systems. She liked systems.

Sam Aarons came into the shop with two cups of coffee in her hand. Sam believed in dressing for the part, wearing flowy skirts and white peasant blouses. Her long, curly red hair topped off the look. She came up to the counter and handed one of the drinks to Rarity. "Hey, neighbor. How did your book club go last night?"

"Didn't your crystals already tell you?" Rarity took a long sip of the coffee. "This is just what I needed. Why is coffee from a shop so much better than what you brew at home?"

"Because Annie brews it with love. At least that's what her sign above the coffee bar says. And my crystals don't tell the future. For that, you need to go to Madame Zelda's next door. She'd be glad to tell you what's going to happen in your future. I just give you the gems to protect yourself from bad juju. Like the clear quartz I sent you when you were diagnosed. It's a master healer stone."

Rarity reached up for the necklace she still wore. "I love it. Even if it didn't cure me."

"You of little faith. Anyway, is the fact that you have a display up for the group a good sign? Lots of attendees?" Sam picked up one of the books and glanced at the back.

Rarity shook her head and held up a finger.

"Why do you want me to wait?" Sam set the book down. "Why can't you tell me now?"

Rarity silently took a drink and waited for Sam to get the message.

"Oh, I get it. But you have got to be kidding me. *One* person showed up? What a waste of time." Sam nodded to the chairs. "Can we sit for a bit? These boots are new and horribly uncomfortable. My feet will be killing me long before I close the shop today."

"What we do for our image. Sorry, of course we can sit." Rarity crossed over and sat in the same chair she'd occupied last night. "It wasn't a complete waste of time. The woman who came brought in a big order, so at least there's that."

"Are you doing okay with the store financially? Walk-in traffic will start picking up soon. Summers can be a little slow. People don't realize it's not going to be as hot as they think here."

Rarity nodded. Business had been slower than she'd hoped, especially since it had taken longer to remodel the building than she'd planned. She'd only been open a few months. "I'll be fine. Tell me about your date last night. How did it go?"

"Do I have to?" Sam groaned and then sipped her coffee.

Rarity giggled. "That bad?"

"We met at the restaurant in Flagstaff because he couldn't drive all this way on a work night. Then he was almost an hour late. He was all Brooks Brothers suit and tie. And he insisted on splitting the bill. Just so no one would feel obligated for anything après dinner." Sam rolled her shoulders. "I'm never going to find Mr. Right. I should just give up the search."

"You're perfect the way you are, and if there's a Mr. Right in your future, he'll find you." Rarity leaned back. "Or we could ask Madame Zelda."

"You are so bad." Sam leaned her head back and closed her eyes. When she spoke, she let her voice waver, imitating the fortune teller. "You will meet a man where you least expect to meet him. He will be tall, dark, and handsome. Please hand over your credit card for payment."

The bell over the door sounded, and Madame Zelda walked into the store.

Rarity stood and hit Sam's arm to alert her as she hurried past. "Madame Zelda, so nice of you to visit. What can I help you with?"

Madame Zelda narrowed her eyes and stared at Sam, who was now also standing but by the fireplace. "I came in to see if you had a flyer for your survivors' club. I have a client who might be interested in some social interaction around the subject matter. She's very timid, though, and I might not be able to get her to come."

"We're a small group so," Rarity added *of two* silently, "so she should feel comfortable." She picked up a flyer from the counter, writing the book list on the front. Then she handed it to the fortune teller. "I'm sure she'd enjoy the discussion. These are the five books that we're considering reading."

"Hey, Rarity, I need to go open. I'll chat with you tonight." Sam circled around the furniture and Madame Zelda and almost ran out of the store.

"That girl needs to relax. She's wound up like a clock ready to bust a spring." Madame Zelda watched Sam through the window as she hurried to open her store. "It's not healthy to be that anxious."

"Sam's a little high-strung." I nodded to the flyer. "I hope your client decides to visit at least once. Can I have her name?"

"I do not divulge my clients' information. Surely you can understand the privacy needed for a job like mine." She tucked the flyer into a pocket on her dress and left the shop.

Rarity waited for her to disappear out of view of the window before responding. "As if people who visit fortune tellers are expecting privacy like it was their doctor. Maybe that's just life in Sedona."

Rarity didn't have time to think about Madame Zelda's privacy policy much more that day because she had several customers show up, one after the other. A few took a flyer about the book club, others asked her to order a book for them, and one walked through the bookstore checking out the stock, and just left.

When she went to lock the door at five, she glanced outside at the empty sidewalk. Or almost-empty sidewalk. The man who'd been window-shopping at her store sat on a bench on the other side of the street reading. He must have felt her stare because he looked up from his book and nodded after meeting her gaze.

Now she felt stupid. He'd just been killing time. Or looking for his online ordering shopping list. Maybe opening a brick-and-mortar store in a digital age hadn't been the smartest idea with the book world changing in front of her eyes.

It didn't matter, though. This was her dream, and she wasn't going to waste any time worrying about opening at the right time. Action was rewarded. Worrying never did anyone any favors.

She went back to the storeroom and grabbed her purse out of the small closet. Then she checked the back door to make sure it was locked. Finally, she turned off the lights, and holding her keys in one hand, went to the front door to leave and then lock up.

The man on the bench was gone when she turned and dropped her keys into her tote. She glanced up and down the street but didn't see him.

"Hey, are you ready? The restaurant's this way." Sam stood outside her shop, waiting for Rarity to join her.

She shook off the vague unease she felt, but before she went to meet her friend, she reached back and checked again that the shop was locked. Then she slowly walked the few steps to meet Sam.

"Everything all right?" Sam's face echoed the fear that Rarity had felt when she'd seen the guy watching her.

Rarity took her arm. "Everything's fine. I'm just hungry, that's all."

Chapter 2

When next Tuesday rolled around, Rarity worked on a crossword puzzle while she waited to see who would show up for the book club. She looked up when the bell sounded over the door. But it was just Sam with a tray filled with cookies and slices of coffee cake.

"I'm happy to pick this up at Annie's, but I think you ordered way too much. What if no one shows?" Sam set the cookies on the wood bar that served as the cash register area. "You only had one person attend last week."

"Don't jinx it. Shirley said she'd be back this week, and she took flyers for her oncologist's office. Besides, if no one shows, then I have a lot of cookies to eat. I won't have to cook dinner for days." Rarity pulled up a stool behind the counter and sat down. She wasn't at her strongest yet, and more often than not, a day at the shop had her falling asleep in her chair after dinner. When she talked to her doctor about her lack of energy, she'd been told to give it time. She was going to use the same mantra for her new book club. "The group will fill out, eventually. This survivors' group is a community service project."

Sam came around, pulled a water bottle out of the fridge, and set it in front of Rarity. "Drink this. You'll feel better if you're hydrated."

"Yes, Mother." Rarity smiled to soften the blow. Besides, Sam was right. She needed to drink more water. Moving to the high desert from the Midwest had made her crave water. She just needed to get better at reading her physical needs. "What are you doing tonight?"

"Since I don't have to be back at the shop until Thursday, I thought I'd grab some takeout and stream that new romance movie everyone's talking about. Hopefully, I'll crash early. Tomorrow, I'm going for a hike. There's a new shop down the street, and the owner is hot. He's leading a

Wednesday morning hike. And surprise, I signed us both up." She put a card on the counter. "It starts at six, and we'll be back at nine. Your shop doesn't open until ten, right?"

"Yes, but I've got inventory tomorrow." Rarity pushed the card back toward her friend. "Don't tell me you paid in advance."

"Yes, I did. And I don't get my money back if we don't show, so be at that address at six." Sam pushed the card back in front of Rarity, with a smile. "You'll be fine. It's not a long trek, and the scenery really is worth the time."

"The hot instructor scenery or the outdoor scenery?" She picked up the card and looked at it. She'd been meaning to start exercising outdoors rather than just walking on her treadmill, but it all seemed too much.

"Both." Sam headed to the door. "See you tomorrow."

A couple of women walked into the bookstore as Sam walked out. Rarity grabbed the card and tucked it into her jeans pocket. "Feel free to look around. I'll be here to answer any questions."

But instead of looking at the bookshelves, the women moved to the register. The younger of the two dropped her voice to almost a whisper. "We're here for the survivors' club? I have my hospital bill with me if I need to prove that I actually had cancer."

"You don't need to prove anything." Rarity came around the counter. "I'm Rarity Cole, and I am the owner of The Next Chapter. I'm also a breast cancer survivor. I'm excited to have you both here."

"I'm Holly Harper and this is Malia Overstreet. We were in the same chemo pod last summer. We both love to read, so naturally we became best friends." Holly put her arm around Malia. "Malia even helped me find an apartment when I had to move out of my house. Divorces are so hard, right?"

"I've never been married, so I'm not sure." Rarity didn't mention the long-term live-in boyfriend who had left when she'd lost her hair. Of course, she rarely mentioned Kevin. Or thought about him anymore. Which was a blessing. "We've got fifteen minutes before the meeting starts, so if you want to look around or go grab a seat by the fireplace, I'll be over there in a few minutes."

"Thanks." Holly pointed to the romance section that was marked off with a heart-shaped sign. "Malia, I'll be over there."

Malia nodded but then just followed Holly to the area. She ran a finger over the books' spines as she glanced through the authors.

It was a habit that Rarity shared with the quiet Malia. Touching the book covers as she looked through a stack. She hoped Malia would start talking during the meeting or this was going to be a very long two hours.

She moved the cookies over to the table near the window and brought out the coffeepot and lemonade pitcher. In a couple of months, if sales kept increasing, she'd hire a second bookseller to work the store while she ran the meeting. But for now, she was chief cook and bottle washer. Which meant she had to do both.

The door opened again, and this time it was Shirley with another woman. Rarity waved at her, and the fifty-something blonde hurried over to her, friend in tow.

"Rarity, this is Kim. She's just starting her journey, but she's going to be a survivor, I can tell. Can she sit in on the meeting?" Shirley hugged Rarity like they'd been separated for years, not just a week.

Welcome to the sisterhood. The cost of joining was just living through a disease that tried to kill you. And you had to wear pink for the rest of your life. (A rule that Rarity ignored since she hated pink.)

Rarity hadn't wanted the group to include current patients, mostly because a lot of times, they didn't know what to think or feel yet. Rarity had tried to make friends with other patients during her treatment, but when she did, it hadn't turned out well. She'd met a woman for dinner after treatment one week, but all the other woman wanted to talk about was how horrible her medical care had been and Rarity's estate plan.

Talking about death like it was inevitable was not a good way to move to a positive attitude about the process. Especially on the first meeting. However, Shirley was so excited about bringing someone, Rarity couldn't bring herself to say no. "Kim, I'm glad to have you, but you might find a current treatment support group is more helpful. We're only a book club."

Kim shook her head. Her blond hair was cut into a cute curtain bangs look. Rarity's hair was coming back in curlier than before, so she'd never be able to pull off that look. "I know I'm not a survivor, yet. But I'm going to be. And you all will give me the strength to keep fighting. Besides, I love reading. What better way to spend my time than at a book club?"

"We're glad to have you." Rarity decided she could deal with the fallout later. If Kim wasn't feeling the group, it wasn't like she would be forced to stay. And tonight, Rarity needed people in the seats. If only to eat all the treats she'd ordered. "Go get some refreshments, and we'll be starting in a little while."

Rarity watched as the group of four moved into the sitting area by the fireplace. Tonight the weather was still warm, so she wouldn't be turning on the gas fire, but she could see them using it in the winter months. As long as the book club continued. Rarity shook off the thought, determined to be positive.

She finished up a few things at the counter and stacked the books she and Shirley had chosen onto the coffee table. She was just about to sit down and call the group to order when a middle-aged woman opened the door to the shop and peeked inside. "Come on in. We're just getting set up for a book club meeting."

The woman looked surprised to be seen, and at first, Rarity thought she was going to shut the door and run, but instead, she swallowed and came inside. She held a clutch purse in front of her like a shield. "Is this the cancer group?"

"Survivors' book club, yes. Sounds like you're in the right place. Do you want some coffee or a snack?" Rarity walked over toward her and held out her hand. "I'm Rarity Cole, bookstore owner and cancer survivor."

"Martha. Martha Redding." She shook Rarity's hand with a limp grip. She wore no jewelry except a ring that had a nice-sized diamond in the middle. "Coffee would be nice."

Rarity pointed over to the table by the window. "Grab a cup and a couple of cookies."

Martha walked away toward the coffee, and Rarity moved a sign into the aisle. She'd had it made earlier that week. It read, BOOK CLUB IN PROGRESS. FEEL FREE TO BROWSE. MEET ME AT THE COUNTER AND RING THE BELL IF YOU WANT TO BUY ANYTHING. Brief and to the point. It was time for week two of the book club to start.

* * * *

Rarity stood in front of the group. "So nice to see everyone tonight. I want us to go around and introduce ourselves. Include what you want to share, but keep it brief for tonight. We've got a lot to get through. I'll be making notes for my own use, and if you'd add a few things, I'd appreciate it. I need your birthday, month and day only, please. As well as any allergies. I hate to bring peanut butter cookies if you're allergic. Oh, and the best book you read last year. That should get us started."

Shirley raised her hand. "I'll start since I was here last week."

Rarity hid a smile as she wrote down Shirley's details. The woman just had to remind everyone that she'd been the first. After she was done, Rarity nodded to Kim, who was sitting next to Shirley. "Kim?"

"I can go last since I'm new." She glanced around the room, but the others just nodded, encouraging her to continue. "Okay, well, I'm Kim. I'm going through treatment now. I'm not allergic to anything. And the best book I've read lately was a vampire romance. I know, cheesy, but I loved it."

"We don't judge anyone on their reading choices. However, I'm not much of a romance reader. I had an unfortunate incident when I started treatment." Rarity looked up. "You forgot your birthday."

"Oh, sorry, May 28." Kim rattled off.

"The twins." Rarity wrote down the info by Kim's name.

Kim frowned. "Excuse me?"

"Gemini, the twins?" Rarity glanced up to see Kim's face. She looked clueless.

"Oh, yeah. I'm not much into horoscopes." Kim broke Rarity's gaze.

"You should be," Malia added. "It will help you so much with scheduling your treatments."

Holly put a hand on Malia's arm. "You'll have to forgive my woo-woo friend. She believes in checking what your horoscope says before getting dressed in the morning."

"I didn't get sick once during treatment because I listened to the stars." Malia rolled her eyes and looked away from her friend. Apparently, they'd had this argument before.

"Anyway, my name is Holly, and I'm a cancer survivor." She stopped and looked around the room. Waving her arms, she leaned forward, expecting a response from the group. When none came, she groaned. "Come on, guys, this is where you say, 'Hi, Holly!' At least that's the way the twelve-step groups do it."

Martha raised her hand. "I thought this was a book club."

Rarity stepped in before Martha decided to run out the door. "It is a book club, Holly was just being funny. Go on, Holly. Tell us a bit about you and your favorite book."

After Holly spoke, Malia rattled off her information faster than Rarity could write it all down. She didn't want to embarrass her and ask her to say things a second time. She'd grab her after the meeting. Rarity glanced around the room. Everyone had spoken, except Martha. Rarity turned to the woman. "So, what brings you here, Martha?"

"That's my business. Look, I'm here to talk about books, not myself. I really don't have a sob story to tell, anyway. I'm a widow and live alone." She pointed to the books on the table. "When are we talking about those?"

"I realize everyone joins book clubs for different reasons, but this one is a little different. We've all been through a life-changing event. I can respect your need for privacy, but you may want to consider if this is the right group for you. We will be talking about what we have in common.

A lot." Rarity put her pen down. "But you're right, it's time to choose our book. Let's vote, and the one with the most votes will be this month's choice. And we also need to determine if we're meeting once a week, we might read two books a month and save one meeting for catching up and choosing another book."

"Tell us why you don't like reading romance," Holly leaned forward. "If that's not too personal."

She'd just told Martha that this was a place to share, so she couldn't blow off Holly's question. Live by the sword, die by the sword. She took a deep breath. "Okay, then. I was engaged at the time I was diagnosed. Kevin, that was his name, he didn't take my situation well. He didn't like it when I was tired or had appointments scheduled that affected his plans. He never even came to a chemo treatment with me. A month after I started treatments, he dumped me and moved out. So, romance isn't my favorite type of reading material." She smiled at the group. "At least not yet."

"Fair enough. I was married to the wrong guy when I went through treatment, so that's why Malia's friendship meant so much. I was able to have someone to talk to." Holly smiled in the general direction of her friend. "Besides, I want to open my reading world a little."

It took another thirty minutes to choose the book and make a plan for how far each person would be able to read before the next week's meeting. Holly stood and got the cookie plate and walked it around to everyone while they chatted. Rarity noticed that most of the group members were starting to bond. Except for Martha.

As they were finishing the group and buying the books, Martha stood first in line to check out. After she'd paid for the book, she hurried out the door. Malia was the next one up in line. She turned and watched Martha climb into her Jeep parked outside next to the large window. "She's still hurting. The treatments affect us all differently. Some people lock all their feelings up inside and don't let others see them. It's like they're convinced they're going to die anyway, so why put others through the pain."

Rarity thought about Malia's comments as she locked up the store and slipped the cookies into a plastic sack. Then she put the sack into her tote along with her copy of the Barbara O'Neal book they'd chosen to read first. *How to Bake a Perfect Life* seemed like an easy choice to get the group started on their new journey.

She set the alarm and locked the front door, shaking the doorknob to make sure it was locked. She didn't think anyone would steal books, but they could make a mess while they searched for something of value to pawn. She turned down the street and walked toward home.

The night was warm, but the overwhelming heat of the day was gone. It was like living in summer year-round. Sometimes she didn't even remember what month it was until she checked the date on her computer as she worked on bookstore business.

The streetlamps that lined Main Street were already on, and Rarity could see the televisions on through the windows of houses she walked past. She hadn't met many of her neighbors on this street. They all either worked out of town, or were retirees who were busy with their own lives. She hadn't known any of her neighbors when she'd lived in St. Louis, either. The days of the neighborhood block party were probably over. People didn't gather because of their proximity. Now they gathered because of shared experiences. Like her new book club.

All thoughts were leading back to Martha's outburst. Why would she have even decided to come to the group if she didn't want to talk to others about their shared experience, cancer? At least Rarity thought Martha might be back. She'd bought the book they'd chosen for the month, Maybe she thought she'd finish the O'Neil book sooner than next week's meeting. Rarity wasn't sure Martha would like the more paranormal woman's fiction, *Magical Midlife Dating* by KE Greene, but she knew Holly and Malia would love it.

Anyway, Martha seemed committed to the reading part of the group, even if she didn't want to share more personal thoughts. Rarity pushed the worries about the book club away as she walked up the sidewalk to her new home.

Rarity's new home was a small sunshine-yellow cottage near the edge of town. It had cost more than she'd expected to pay, mostly because any property inside city limits was seen as having a possible commercial value. But the prior owners had taken care of the two-bedroom cottage and its outdoor area. She missed her grass yard, but the backyard deck with a hot tub and a bonus lap pool had been worth the extra money.

Tonight, she planned to pour an extra-large glass of wine and slip on her swimsuit. She put a frozen dinner that she'd made herself a few weeks ago into the oven, poured her wine, then went to change. Cooking a few times a month, she had frozen a few weeks' worth of meals for evenings like this when she was drained from work. Taking a towel and the wine out to the deck, she turned on the pool lights and went down the stairs to swim away the tension in her neck.

Later, after she'd eaten and poured a second glass of wine, this one a little smaller, she opened the hot tub and set an alarm on her phone. She set the phone out of arm's reach and slipped into the hot water, letting the jets massage away the rest of the tightness.

As she relaxed, she thought about the women in her new group. Would they all stay? Right now, she had doubts about Kim and Martha. Kim, because she would probably become overwhelmed with the book club and the discussions. Rarity mused as she swirled the wine in the glass, letting the lights sparkle inside the liquid, considering that Martha's exit would also stem from her being overwhelmed.

One would be trying to learn to live while dying, the other trying to stop dying when she was living.

Life was hard. Rarity closed her eyes as she let her body relax into the water and the night. Living after having believed you were dying was even harder.

Chapter 3

Rarity's alarm went off at five the next morning. She stared, bleary eyed, at the numbers on the clock. It must be a mistake. She didn't get up this early. Had someone come in and changed her wakeup times?

Then she remembered. Sam's hike. She dragged herself out of bed and went to stand under her rain-forest showerhead. She could swim before opening the store this morning. Or wait until after she got home. The one thing she wasn't going to do was let the pool sit, unused. She'd sacrificed square footage in the cottage to get the house with the pool and still come in reasonably under budget.

When she was ready, she grabbed a backpack and put a couple of water bottles inside as well as a few protein bars. Smoothing sunscreen over any exposed part of her body, she tucked that bottle inside the backpack, as well. She pulled on a ball cap that showed her love of a certain football team that had its home base in Dallas. She'd been a Rams fan, like most of St. Louis, until they'd moved away from the Gateway city. Then she had to change her allegiance.

She felt like she was doing the same thing now. Finding out who and what she was now that she lived in Sedona.

She made it to the hiking shop with ten minutes to spare. Annie's Bakery was across the street, and Rarity wondered if she had time to grab some coffee to push away the cobwebs from that unwise second glass of wine last night.

"Rarity, there you are." Sam hurried toward her with two large coffees in hand. "I can't believe you actually came."

She took the cup from Sam and took a sip before speaking. "I really need to figure out how to read you. I didn't realize not showing up was an option. Thanks for the coffee, though."

"You're welcome. I figured you'd stay up late after your book club thing." Sam sat on a planter box that had been filled with gravel. No flowers in front of this shop. "Come sit and tell me what happened. Was it just you and Shirley again?"

"No. I actually had five people show up. Six if you count me." Rarity told her about the women who'd shown up and their stories. She left Martha for last. After she'd told her everything, she turned toward Sam. "Do you know this Martha Redding? Maybe she has a story?"

Sam shook her head and then drained her coffee. "No, sorry. I have no idea who she is. Maybe she'll connect with people and open up more as the weeks go by. Sometimes people don't open up well in crowds."

"You can hardly call a group of six a crowd. But you might be right." Rarity threw away her now-empty cup. She eyed the bakery. "Do you think I have time to run over there and grab a second cup? Do you want one?"

"No, and no. You need to be here or our hiking guide will leave you behind. He's been known to do it."

Rarity grinned at her friend. "You say that like it would be a bad thing."

"Ha-ha." Sam pointed across the small crowd that had gathered to a bus that pulled up in front of the tour shop. It was an old school bus with *ENDER'S TOURS* painted on the side. "There's our ride. He's got our names on a list. Come on. We're heading out to the Cathedral Rock area. You're going to feel the vortex, I just know it."

Rarity tried not to roll her eyes, but a fellow hiker caught her. The older man laughed and pointed to the woman next to him.

"My wife's just the same. All this mumbo jumbo when all I want is a good hike." He held out his hand. "Jonathon Anderson, and my wife's name is Edith. Are you here visiting with your friend?"

"Rarity Cole. Actually, I just moved here. My friend's name is Sam, she runs the crystal shop in town. I've got the bookstore next door. I haven't been able to do much sightseeing since I've been getting the store up and going." She shook his hand.

He stepped closer to her as they moved toward the bus entrance. "Tell me, do you carry any Tom Clancy in that store? Or is it all the new age stuff my wife buys?"

"I've got a full section of mystery, thrillers, and spy novels. You should come by. I'm sure you'll find something to read, and so will your wife. I'm curating a section of alternate healing topics." Rarity leaned closer and whispered, "It was in my contract for the business license. I'm also required to carry at least a few books on alien visitation and Roswell."

He laughed, but then paused when he saw her face. "You're joking, right?"

Rarity smiled. "I guess you won't know until you visit my store."

"That's one way to get people in the door." He helped his wife up the steps into the bus. "Are you open later today?"

"Ten to six." She paused at the driver, who had the clipboard. "I'm Rarity Cole."

"Thank you." The driver made a mark by her name. "Archer Ender at your service. I understand you're our newest business owner in town."

"I opened The Next Chapter downtown." She took a step, then stopped. "If you need guidebooks of the area, I'd be glad to carry them for your customers."

"That's not a bad idea." Archer nodded to the back. "We'd better table this, or we're going to miss our window to see the best wildlife."

The woman next in line took a step closer, forcing Rarity to step into the main cabin of the bus.

"Sorry, you're right." Rarity scanned the bus and found Sam sitting near the back. She hurried over and sat next to her. "You left me."

"You snooze, you lose. Besides, I wanted to sit in the back. Archer needs new shocks on this thing so it's bumpier back here." Sam bounced on the seat.

"And that's a good thing?" Rarity caught Archer looking back at her and met his gaze. Which he quickly dropped. As she settled in next to Sam, she wondered what Archer's story was. Single? In a relationship? She focused on Sam's chatter and tried to keep her mind off the handsome man who was driving them out to the desert.

Rarity had to admit, the hike was breathtaking. The heat, on the other hand, was overwhelming. She was used to St. Louis summers, but she'd dealt with the high heat and humidity by staying inside at the worst of the days. Here, she was purposely out hiking in the madness. But the view was totally worth it.

She looked over and saw Archer standing near the edge. The overlook site was fenced off, but even with that, every tour she'd been on, some kid had to show off and put themselves in danger. She pulled out a bottle of cold water and a power bar from the bag she'd packed earlier. Archer had offered her water when she'd gotten off the bus so apparently she hadn't needed to bring her own. Better to be prepared than thirsty, she mused. She sipped her water and sat on one of the metal benches where she could see across the valley.

"That's Cathedral Rock to your left." Archer pointed to the large red rock formation as he sat on the bench next to her with his water bottle in hand. "Sensitive types swear they can feel the vortex as soon as we come into a few miles of the area. I appreciate the mythology, but really, I just enjoy the view."

"I have to say I agree with you." Rarity looked over and saw Sam chatting with Jonathon and his wife. "Just don't tell Sam. She'll be disappointed that the vortex didn't course through my body, healing all the dead cells and rejuvenating new ones."

"A physical trainer would tell you that's the power of getting up off your butt to see the rocks in the morning, not the vortex itself." He smiled as he leaned up against the backrest of the bench. "I should stop telling people my secret, or no one will book my tours. You're not sick, are you? When I was having breakfast at the diner last week, I heard you opened a book club with an odd focus."

"Not really odd. Just a different perspective." She smiled and decided to share a little with this complete stranger. No matter what the subject started with, as soon as someone found out that she'd survived cancer, they wanted to talk about their miraculous recovery from the disease. Or a friend who had died. It never failed. "I had cancer last year. I'm good now, but it makes you reconsider things."

"I bet. Sorry if I was making light of your situation." He stood. "I guess I'd better get this hike going again. I know you have a bookstore to open."

And with that he was gone.

On the bus on the way back, Rarity saw a familiar person on the street. She nudged Sam and then pointed out the window. "That's Martha Redding. Right there in the parking lot of the grocery store."

Sam turned so she could see the woman. "From last night? Is she in the pink shorts and print shirt?"

"That would be her. Look, she has dog food in her cart. Maybe I can use that to try to get her to bond next week. We can talk about our pets."

Sam turned and looked at her. "Except you don't have a pet."

"Not yet. I wanted to get settled again. I think it's time to hit the humane society this weekend. I suppose there's not one in Sedona, right?"

"Sorry, no. But I know a breeder or two. Goldendoodles are really popular, and they aren't supposed to shed." Sam pulled out her phone and started looking up contacts.

"I'd rather have a rescue. I'd like to be feeling like I'm saving someone from a kill shelter."

Sam keyed something into her phone. "There's a shelter in Flagstaff, and they are open at eight on weekdays. You should be able to get there and back before opening the shop."

"Then that's what I'm going to do tomorrow. I've been thinking about this way too long. It's time to act." She saw the tour company's office coming up on the right side of the road. "Time to get ready for work. Stop by tonight and I'll make dinner."

"Sorry, I've got a thing tonight." Sam didn't meet her gaze.

"Don't tell me you're going on another date from your online match program?" Rarity wasn't sure if she'd ever date again, but she knew it wouldn't be a guy some computer thought she'd be perfect for.

Sam blushed. "Actually, that couple I was talking to at the overlook. They invited me to have dinner with them and their son. They're here visiting him. He lives here."

"Are you sure? I mean, Jonathon didn't mention a son to me when we were talking. Don't go somewhere secluded where they can cut out your kidney to sell on the black market." Rarity adjusted her tote and stood, waiting for Sam to stand and exit the bus.

"Way to make me feel all warm and cozy about my night." Sam peered at the couple through the windows as they waved at her. They took off walking down the strip, arm in arm. "They look normal, don't they?"

Rarity laughed. "I was just kidding, but if you feel like something's off, call me. I'll come rescue you."

"I'll be at Café Ole at seven. I'll call you after we're seated. If you don't hear from me by eight, call." Sam stepped off the bus and started walking toward their shops. "Thanks for making me paranoid."

"A little paranoia is a good thing." Rarity waved at Archer, who was watching them from the driver's seat. "A girl can't be too careful."

* * * *

Rarity didn't get to the dog shelter the next morning. She met Sam for breakfast at Annie's Bakery instead.

"How did the dinner go?"

"I had a wonderful time talking with the Andersons. Jonathon is a retired New York City cop. They are traveling the country visiting their kids before they decide where to finally settle down. They're here for the next few months. And their son, Drew, didn't show up." Sam poured sugar into her coffee and stirred. "Edith was embarrassed, but I told her that I enjoyed their company just as much as if her son had been there."

"At least you were able to keep your kidney." Rarity sipped her coffee and waved at a woman leaving the shop with a box of donuts. "That's Holly Harper. She's one of my book club members. From what I remember, she got divorced either in treatment or just after."

"I can't believe anyone would divorce someone who's going through treatment. What about the "til death do us part' vow?"

"Well, it's better to figure out who a person is sooner than later." Rarity thought about Kevin and his decision to continue playing league basketball with his friends once she'd started treatment. She could barely heat up food, let alone cook, yet he'd been out of the house two sometimes three nights a week. Sam had been her rock during that time. Even living fourteen hundred miles away. "Did I ever thank you for your help during my treatment?"

"If I'd been really helpful, I would have come and kicked Kevin to the curb months before he actually left." Sam squeezed Rarity's hand. "That's why you always need to keep your friends close. To take out the trash when needed."

Rarity smiled as the waitress brought them their plates of quiche. It was good to have friends.

* * * *

Tuesday came sooner than she'd expected, and Rarity was still reading the book when Shirley stepped into the bookstore at six thirty. Rarity held up a hand when she heard the door open. "I'm over here."

"And I disturbed you. I am so sorry. I'll just sit here and work on my baby blanket. I got so involved in the book, I didn't get much done this week. That baby will be here before I get this done."

"Coffee and treats are on the table." Rarity went back to reading, knowing that Shirley would make herself at home and be perfectly content with someone reading rather than talking. That was the cool thing about readers. They got each other.

Rarity finished the last chapter and set the book aside with a sigh. It had been a strong romance with woman's fiction elements rather than a true women's fiction, but for once, Rarity hadn't minded. The hero was solid. And the heroine did the work to make herself strong. Someone whom Rarity would want to be friends with. Maybe that was the hook for the discussion tonight. The power of friendship, especially when people were going through a bad time. Like dealing with cancer.

The rest of the group showed up right at seven. Rarity pulled over the sign near the door, then looked out the door to see if Martha was on her way. The man she'd seen last week was sitting on the bench. He waved a hand when he saw her and Rarity waved back.

She closed the door and went in to sit by the fireplace. "Did anyone talk to Martha last week? I saw her on Wednesday doing some shopping."

Shirley shook her head. "I've seen her in town before last week, but I didn't know her. And I didn't see her at all last week."

The other women shook their heads as well. Kim raised her hand. "Did she give you her phone number?"

Rarity laughed. "Martha barely gave us her name. I'll can reach out to her tomorrow and see if she wants to continue with the group. I mean, you're not required to come, but I'd like to make sure she's okay."

"So maybe we should have each other's phone numbers, just in case we can't be here one night. That way we can call someone else, and no one will have to worry about us." Shirley grabbed her phone from her purse. Then she looked at Kim. "Call this number, 928-555-5555. That's me. And I'll answer and put you in my contacts. Then everyone else call me one at a time."

"Or we could just put The Next Chapter's number in everyone's phone and you'll all have it. Then if you're not coming, just give me a call or leave a message. That way we won't worry." Rarity wrote the number to the shop on the flip chart she'd brought out for tonight's discussion. "And we don't have to spend a lot of time on a phone tree. There's a lot to talk about with this book tonight. I thought we could start with friendship. What did you think of the main character's hesitation to let her friends into her world?"

As the discussion continued, Rarity was pleasantly surprised that she didn't have to guide the conversation very much at all. Everyone took a turn and was supportive of the group. Ideas built on each other until they ran out of time. And still, Rarity watched the group's members continue to chat as they left the shop. It had been a successful night.

The next morning, Rarity called Sam. "You don't know anyone who might have Martha's phone number, do you?"

"No. I don't know anyone who's ever talked to her before," Sam responded. "However, there is a welfare check line you can call and leave the information. Just let them know that she didn't show up for a book club meeting and the group was worried."

"You don't think that's a little overkill? What if she just decided not to come back? She wasn't very happy with me or the group last week," Rarity reminded her friend.

"So? You can't make her madder than she already is if she's just ghosted you. And it might teach her some manners." Sam rattled off a number. "Call and report her. You won't let this go until you do."

That was true. Sam knew her too well. "Okay. I'll let you know what I find out."

Rarity left a message on the machine explaining who she was and why she was calling. Then she went on with her day. By the time she arrived at the bookstore, the man on the bench was back. He stood when she started unlocking the bookstore and she held the door open for him. "Dying to get the next book in a series?"

He smiled and pulled out a card. "Actually, I'm Drew Anderson, Sedona Police Department. I wanted to talk to you about Martha Redding."

Chapter 4

Rarity flipped on the lights, then went to the counter to stash her tote. She pointed to the sofa near the fireplace. "Let's sit down. Did something happen to Martha? Is she okay? Did someone take her kidney?"

"Wait, what?" He followed her to the sitting area and pulled out a notebook. "No one took her kidney, at least, we can't confirm that happened. Why...do you ask?"

"Sorry, I saw something on television the other night. It was out of Tucson, I think. Or maybe Texas, the show didn't really say. Anyway, there's this gang that sends someone out to get to know you, then you wake up in a bathtub in a pile of ice." She perched on the edge of the chair and took a breath. "I'm surprised you guys weren't alerted to the issue."

"I don't think it's a real issue. That's been an urban legend for years." He pointed to the flip chart. "Whose number is that?"

"The store's. The group was worried when Martha didn't show up last night. Well, she wasn't very happy with the idea of having to talk about personal things, so there was a chance she just decided to drop the club. It happens. But the group wanted to have a way for us to alert each other if someone wouldn't be able to attend. So, they're going to call in 'sick' if they can't come." She paused, thinking about last night. "But you were out there on the bench last night. Watching the bookstore. You already knew that Martha was missing."

He studied her and then nodded. "We found this book club event in her appointment book when we searched her house. When she didn't show up last night, we started checking out other avenues. When you called for a welfare check, I wondered if you knew more."

"I don't understand. Why did you search her house?" Rarity was getting a bad feeling about this entire thing. People didn't just go missing from Sedona, did they? It was a small town—less than twenty thousand people—at least that was the number claimed on the city website. Rarity had studied Sedona carefully, including its crime rate and city structure, before she'd cashed out some of her deferred comp to buy the bookstore and her house.

"We had a barking dog complaint on Sunday. When no one answered the door, we worried she might have been in danger. There wasn't anyone in the house besides the dog." He glanced around the bookstore. "Was Mrs. Redding a frequent customer?"

Rarity shook her head. "Actually, I'd never met her before last week. She came to the last meeting. She bought the book and left. Actually, as grumpy as she was to the group, I wasn't sure she was coming back."

"She was grumpy? Was there an altercation? Did one specific person seem to have any issues with Mrs. Redding?" Now Drew Anderson was interested in her story.

"She didn't want to talk about personal things. This is a cancer survivors' group. Everything we talk about is personal. She didn't get in a fight with anyone. I just think she wasn't comfortable sharing information about her personal life." Rarity sank into the chair. "I can't believe she's missing. What did you do with her dog?"

Drew looked up sharply. "What did you just ask?"

"What did you do with the dog? You didn't leave it at the house alone, did you?" Rarity saw the answer in his eyes. "Oh, no. You did. Did anyone at least stop by and feed it?"

"We're not evil, Ms. Cole. Of course, someone is feeding the dog. I stopped by yesterday to walk through the house one more time. I think, though, we're going to have to take it to Flagstaff tomorrow if someone doesn't show up to care for it." He closed his notebook. "So if there's not anything else…"

"I will." The words were out of her mouth before she could even ask what kind of dog it was. Big, if the bag of dog food she'd seen in Martha's cart was a clue. She could tell he didn't understand what she was saying. "I'll take care of the dog until Martha comes back or we find out more."

"You barely knew her."

She nodded. "That's true, but if I'm going to be part of this community, I want to do my part when I'm needed. That dog needs me. And I have a big backyard. It will be a good trial for me to care for someone besides myself. What's the dog's name? Do you know?"

"According to his tag, it's Killer." He waited a beat, letting that sink in. "Look, you don't have to do this. No one expects you to take on dog-sitting duties just because you're the newest member of our community. She had to have relatives somewhere."

"So, I'll take Killer until you find Martha or her next of kin." Rarity shivered a bit. The air-conditioning must have been set too high.

"I'll stop by the shop with him and his food just before you close." Drew stood and tucked his notebook away. "My dad said you were a kind soul. I guess he was right."

"Your dad? Don't tell me he's a customer." Rarity racked her brain for an older gentleman who had come into the bookstore recently.

"You met my parents on a hike last week." Drew picked up a book someone had left on the coffee table, then set it back down. "I keep telling them they're going to get hurt out on those trails."

"Oh, yes, Jonathon and Edith. I guess I thought they were tourists." She leaned forward, remembering more about the couple. "Wait, you're the guy who stood up my friend Sam for dinner."

"In my defense, one, I was working. And two, they never told me they'd invited someone. Please tell your friend that I'm sorry they led her astray. I'm not looking for a wife. Or a girlfriend." He turned toward the door. "I'll see you tonight."

"For your information, I don't think Sam is looking for a proposal, just a date. It can get pretty lonely out here. Maybe you should consider making it up to her," Rarity called after him, but Drew just opened the front door and left. "What an idiot. Sam's better off not meeting him."

A few minutes later, the door flew open, and Shirley came hurrying inside. "I can't believe it, can you?"

"I take it you heard about Martha?" Rarity stood at the counter, checking new books into her system before putting them on the shelves. She needed to stop ordering books until she started selling more than she brought in during a week. But she just kept running into books she thought she'd like so she ordered them for the store. It wasn't an exact science.

"I was getting my hair done at the Curl and Dye this morning. Everyone was talking about it, even Pastor Evans's wife, Chloe. And she never gossips about anyone. That's how I knew it was true." Shirley picked up one of the books Rarity had just scanned. "Is this for sale? I've been meaning to read it."

"Of course," Rarity smiled. Shirley and her husband might just keep the bookstore running until she got a solid customer base. "And George's books came in."

"Thank you for reminding me. I forgot last night." Shirley dug in her purse. "He's found four more he needs ordered."

"You guys are my best customers so far." Rarity tucked the list by the cash register. "I feel so bad for Martha. Do you think she's just off visiting someone? Maybe she's just fine, and Drew Anderson's storming around her house for nothing."

"Rarity, I don't know a lot about Martha, but according to Chloe Evans, there's no way she would have left her dog without boarding him somewhere. She loved that dog."

That afternoon, the rest of the Survivors' Club visited the shop to check in with Rarity and see what she thought about Martha's disappearance. Even though everyone said they hadn't known Martha well, they all said the same thing. She wouldn't have left the dog.

It was nearly time to shut down the store, but Rarity still hadn't seen Drew again. She glanced at her watch as her stomach rumbled. She'd been distracted by the people dropping in at the shop to close for lunch, and none of the town's three diners delivered on Wednesdays. Mostly her customers had been a lot of lookers and few buyers. She needed to set up a fridge in the office area and fill it with microwavable dinners and sodas for days like this. Especially since it would be a while before she felt comfortable enough to hire someone to help.

The door opened, and Drew stood there. "Are you ready?"

"I've been waiting for you. Are you going to bring him inside?" Rarity put her tote on the counter.

"I'll drive the two of you home. I picked up some fried chicken and fixings at Carole's for dinner so I hope you like chicken."

She frowned, but quickly pushed past it. He was being nice. That's all. She was doing Martha, and probably him, a big favor. She held up a finger. "Let me double-check the back door and turn off the lights. Just stand there and I'll be right out."

When she came out of the back, he was reading the back cover of a spy novel. Apparently, he had the same taste in books that his dad did. She picked it up off the shelf when he set it back down. "Clancy. He's one of your father's favorites too. Did you know that?"

He nodded. "I wanted to be in the CIA because of all the books Dad had around the house. It's just harder to get an invite than I thought possible. Are we ready?"

She handed him the book. "We are now. Take this as a thank-you for what you're doing for Killer. I know it would have probably been easier to dump him at the humane society."

"I don't run away from problems." He took the book and smiled. "Thanks for this. You didn't need to, but it is thoughtful. I might just have to buy my books here rather than take a trip into Flagstaff." He held the door open for her.

A large Dodge truck sat on the road in front of her shop. A large dog crate was in the back-seat area. Rarity wasn't tall enough to see what was inside. But thinking of adding a new pet, even if just a temporary one, to her life gave her a sense of peace. Like her new roommate was not only meant to be, but that he was going to be one of the best things to happen to her for a long time.

Drew held open the truck door for her and she climbed into the seat. She turned to look at the dog, but the opening was turned away from her. When Drew got into the driver's seat, she put on her seat belt.

"Thanks for the ride home. I typically walk back and forth. I guess that would have been impossible with the dog and his belongings."

"Yeah, Mrs. Redding seemed to have a lot of stuff for one dog. There's wet and dry food, treats, toys, chew bones, you name it. Her place looked like a pet store." He started the truck and pulled into traffic.

"I bet he misses her." Rarity pointed to the street where he needed to turn. "I'm down that way."

"I know where you live. You realize I'm a Sedona police detective, right? I had to do a background check on you before you were approved for a business license. We take security very seriously around here." He turned on a blinker and waited for a car to pass them.

"So, who is Martha's next of kin?"

He turned his head and glanced at her. "What are you talking about?"

"Don't tell me *she* didn't get the background check when she moved in." Rarity glanced out at the windows at the houses with their lights just coming on for the evening. They looked like homes. Rarity's house typically looked like no one lived there. A condition that was going to get her robbed if she didn't change her ways. Anyway, having a dog would help scare away strangers.

"She didn't open a business, so no, we didn't get a background check on her. And she's lived here a long time, so we don't have much information on her family. Which is a problem now." He pulled into her driveway next to her bright red Mini Cooper. The driveway was supposed to be one car wide, like the garage, but Rarity's car was so small, Drew could fit his full-sized truck on the side. He turned off the engine. "I'll help you get everything inside, and then I'll let him out. He's used to seeing me, so maybe it will help the transition. Are you used to dogs?"

"I had one a year ago. My boyfriend had a Boston terrier, but when we split up, the dog went with him." Rarity unlocked the house door and held the door open so Drew could bring in the cage.

He set it in the middle of the floor. "Go make sure all your bedroom doors are shut, as well as any outside doors. We don't want him running away or getting stuck under your bed." He nodded to the front door. "I'll go get the rest of the stuff. Don't let him out until I'm back inside."

"Yes, sir." She gave a quick salute, then ran to shut all the doors. After checking the door to the garage and the one to the deck, she went to the kitchen, got a bowl, and filled it with water.

Then she sat cross-legged on the floor in front of the cage. She leaned against the couch and called the dog to the front of the cage. Nothing happened. "Killer, come here, boy. I want to be your friend. We'll have a happy dog zone. As long as you don't chew up my house while I'm gone, I'll give you whatever you want. Food, water, toys, you name it. How does that sound?"

A whimper came from the back of the cage.

"Oh, buddy, you're scared. It's okay. You're just going to stay with me until they find Martha. Then you'll go back home with your best friend. Maybe I'll come over for a visit if you want."

Drew came in and pointed to the dog food. "Where do you want it?"

"Put it on my counter, the island part. I'll need to find somewhere to put all the food, so he doesn't get up and eat it in the middle of the night. Or while I'm at work." She held out her hand. "Give me one of those bowls, and fill the other one up with dry food. You can bring it over, and maybe he'll feel safe enough to leave the cage." Rarity poured the water from her bowl into one of Killer's dog dishes. She took the second one from Drew when he came back after filling it. "Can you open the cage now?"

"Are you sure that's what you want?" He sat on the floor next to her. "Maybe we should just put the food and drink into the cage—that way you don't have to worry about anything."

"I'm not having a dog in a cage in my house. Pets are part of the family." She glanced over at him, trying to size him up. "Didn't you have pets when you were growing up?"

"The barn cat kept having babies in the barn. My mom would give them all away, and Captain Marvel would have another batch." He blushed. "I haven't told that story in a long time."

"Which part embarrassed you? The one where you cared for a cat or the fact that you named her Captain Marvel?" Drew was getting more and more interesting.

"I loved the comic book. I guess I was hooked on law enforcement early on." He reached out and opened the cage door. "Killer, come on, boy. Come out and meet Rarity. She's going to be taking care of you for a while."

Rarity saw the movement in the back and then a small Yorkshire terrier hurried out of the cage. She wanted to reach out and hug the little guy, but she could see he was shaking and scared. "Hey, Killer, how are you today?"

The dog barked at her, letting the action make him fly up on all four legs.

"Is that so? Do you want some water?" She pushed the bowl a little closer and then met Drew's gaze. "You made him seem a little bigger than he is."

"Big-hearted little fellow. I want to use him to find Martha's kidnapper, but the police chief thinks it's too soon. They think Martha is off on a huge shopping spree and she's just forgotten about her dog. Or maybe she told her daughter, and the girl blew off taking care of the dog." He tapped his fingers on the floor, and Killer came to him.

"Your police chief doesn't have pets. And he's an idiot."

Killer looked up at her when she said that and barked again.

"I think he agrees with you. And since I want to keep my job, I'll leave it at that. Shall we eat?" He stood and dusted off his jeans. "I set the bags in your kitchen."

Killer whined at his feet asking to be picked up. He did and gave the little dog a hug. "Now, you be good for Ms. Rarity. She's going to take good care of you."

"Maybe you should take him." Rarity stood and petted the dog's body. He wasn't shaking as much. He liked Drew. "I'll pull out plates. Maybe we can eat outside so Killer can explore the back yard."

"Sounds good. I would take Killer in a heartbeat, but there's a few problems. I work longer hours than you do. And my folks are staying at my place. My mom's allergic to pet dander. At least that's her story." His buzzer went off, and he checked the display. Then he handed Killer over to Rarity. "Sorry, I've got to go. Enjoy dinner. I'd like to stop by and check on him if you'd let me."

"You're not eating? I could divide some out for you." When he didn't answer, Rarity followed him to the front door. "Please keep me in the loop about finding Martha. I have to say, I'm worried."

"I'll grab something later. After the call. That's the problem with being a small-town cop. You never know when you're going to get to eat." He opened the door and paused. "Look, I'm worried about her too. Anyway, thanks again for taking the dog in. Have a good night, Killer."

Rarity sat on the couch for a few minutes with the dog until the smell of chicken got her attention. She put Killer on the floor and went into the kitchen, where a bag of takeout sat on the counter along with the dog food. "I guess we both need to eat dinner tonight."

Chapter 5

"You're not really going to call this cute little thing 'Killer,' are you?" Sam sat at the bookstore with Killer on her lap. Rarity couldn't bring herself to leave him at the house all alone, so when she'd come into the shop, she'd clicked on his leash, and he'd come trotting after her. Since they'd arrived at the bookstore, he'd been hanging out by the fireplace, where Rarity had set a bowl of water, his dry food, and an assortment of toys she'd brought from home.

"He's not my dog—he's Martha's. I can't very well change his name while she's gone. Maybe she's in the hospital or something like that. I wonder if Drew checked." Rarity finished stocking the last of the books that had come in that morning. She looked around the store. There wasn't much to do. She could go back into the office and pay bills, but that could wait until tomorrow. So she sat on the couch across from Sam.

"According to Edith, Drew has called all the local hospitals. No one matching Martha's description has checked in." She set Killer on the floor. "She said Drew spent a lot of time with you last night."

"Actually, no, he stayed around to see if Killer would settle with me, he even bought dinner, but then he got a call and had to leave." Rarity studied her friend. "Wait, you're not jealous, are you? He was just dropping off the dog."

"And he bought you dinner. Which is more than I could get out of him." Sam waved it off. "Never mind. I'm being silly. I can't even say we've had a first date. It's just been way too long since I had a serious relationship. I thought he might work out. Especially since his parents are so nice."

"Maybe he doesn't want to be set up by his parents." Rarity tossed a ball to Killer, who went running after it. Then he took it back to his spot near the fireplace and lay down to chew on the rubber edges. "Killer doesn't play ball right."

Sam smiled as she reached down and rubbed the dog's ears. "He's his own little man. Who says in his world that isn't the right way to play ball?"

Rarity laughed and curled her feet underneath her. "Is it bad that I don't want them to find Martha right now? I really am enjoying spending time with him. He slept on the extra pillow on my bed last night."

"He's the perfect boyfriend. Maybe I need a Killer in my life instead of a man." Sam glanced at her watch. "I've got to go reopen the shop. I've got a client coming in to talk crystal healing. She's been having some issues with her heart."

"Like in romance, or should you be giving her the name of a cardiologist?" Rarity called after her friend.

"Oh, ye of little faith." Sam paused by the door. "I'm glad you took in the dog. Killer needed you."

After Sam left, Rarity got out her phone and took several pictures of Killer with his ball. He was so cute the way he'd watch her and turn his head like he knew exactly what she was saying. "What on earth did you get yourself into, Rarity? Giving him back to Martha is going to kill you."

The door opened, and Holly and Malia hurried inside. They sat in the same chairs they had during the book club meeting. Holly spoke first. "I can't believe it's true? Shirley called us yesterday after we talked to you, but I still don't believe it."

"Shirley called you? I guess you exchanged numbers?" So much for keeping the members' personal information private.

"Sorry, I know you wanted to avoid us exchanging digits, but we all met at the diner after the meeting and talked. We decided we wanted to be more than just a book group. It's been so long since I've had friends who totally understood me. I lost a lot of them when I told them I had cancer. It was like they thought it was contagious," Holly explained.

"Or that I was going to die in front of them," Malia added. She pointed to Killer, who was still chewing on the ball. "I didn't know you had a dog."

"It's Martha's dog." Rarity took a step back in her head. She hadn't meant to be judgmental. It was just the group was becoming more than what she'd imagined. And it was her group. But that was where she was wrong. She didn't own the group—she was a member, just like the rest of them.

"Oh, then, you found her." Holly pulled out her phone. "Shirley will be so happy. Let me call her."

"Hold on a second. I didn't find her. Drew, he works for the police, he asked me to watch Killer for Martha. Until they find her, that is."

Rarity tried to explain exactly how she'd gotten roped into this mess, but she wasn't quite sure why she'd even volunteered. Killer pawed at her jeans. Automatically she reached down and picked the little dog up and stroked his ears.

"He looks like he's fitting right in." Holly reached out and petted the dog. "I'm glad he's not alone. I've got to go. I'm working tonight."

"What do you do for work?" Rarity liked the way Killer felt in her arms. She was definitely getting a dog when Martha came back and reclaimed this one.

"I'm in computer management for the city. Right now, I'm working a scanning project to transfer all the old police files into digital format. You wouldn't believe how much stuff there is in old paper folders. And while things are uploading, I have time to read. It's awesome." She waved and headed to the door. Malia followed her. "See you on Tuesday."

After they left, a steady stream of people came in and out of the shop. She watched Killer when the doors opened, but he seemed perfectly content to hang around the fireplace, as long as he could see her. When she went to the back to grab a box, she found him at the office door waiting for her to return.

At the end of the day, she went over to the couch and let him jump on her lap. "You're not letting me out of your sight, are you?"

Killer licked her hand and watched her face as she talked—like he was trying to understand the words she was saying.

"They say dogs can understand about three hundred words. I know you know 'food' and 'bed.' Are you up to learning some different words while Martha is away?" She scratched under his chin.

Killer barked, and his entire body flew a few inches off her lap with the effort.

She laughed and snapped his leash on his collar. "Okay, I take that as a yes. Let's go home and get some food."

Rarity picked up her tote and keys and tucked the copy of the dog training book she'd found on the shelves into the tote. She needed to know how to be a good pet owner, even if this first one was a foster kid.

Killer sat at her feet, watching as she finished the last few closing tasks. When she went outside, she found Sam sitting on the bench outside her store. "Hey, what are you doing out here?"

"Waiting for you. There's a café down the street that has outdoor seating, and I called to check. Killer's welcome as long as he's not a barker." She took Rarity's arm. "I felt bad about questioning your night with Drew, so

I thought I'd buy you dinner to say I'm sorry. Girls rule, boys drool. Well, except for Killer."

"He drools when he sleeps. And he snores a bit. I can't promise he's not a barker, though. I don't know him that well," Rarity admitted as they walked down to the café. "Of course, the snoring is so cute, I don't mind it."

"That's what people always say at the beginning of a relationship. Just wait until you two have been together for years. His snoring is going to drive you batty." Sam held the gate open, and they moved to the hostess stand at the restaurant, Sedona Hills.

"You're forgetting that this is a short-term relationship." Rarity picked Killer up so they could walk through the maze of outdoor tables without him bothering anyone.

"For your sake, I'm hoping not." Sam sat at the table and picked up her menu. "Maybe they'll find Martha and she'll decide she doesn't want a dog anymore."

"Best-case scenario," Rarity agreed as a waitress set silverware on their table.

The waitress clucked as she set down water glasses. "I'm assuming you want water? I'm supposed to ask since we're always being reminded we're in a desert. Which is why people want water, but you can't tell my boss that. Anyway, are you talking about that poor woman who went missing this week? Isn't it awful? My boyfriend is a cop, and he says they're worried she went out into the desert to die."

"I'm sure people don't really do that. Isn't that an animal thing?" Rarity stared up at the young woman whose name tag said Jen.

"People are animals. I'm taking classes at the community college. You wouldn't believe how many of our behaviors are due to instinct. Anyway, do you want something besides water?" Jen poised her pen over her notepad.

"Iced tea, no sugar," Rarity responded, and Sam nodded.

Jen wrote the order down, then tucked the notepad away into her apron. "Coming right up. Our special is chef's play on meat loaf. It's really good, but kind of small. And the soup of the day is chicken tortilla. I'll give you some time to look at the menu."

After Jen had left, Sam leaned closer to Rarity. "You don't think that maybe Martha's cancer came back and she *did* go into the desert, do you?"

"Why, so she didn't have to go through treatment again?" Rarity shook her head. "I guess it could be true, but if I was planning my last days and I even tolerated my dog, I wouldn't leave until I had everything in order, including a new home for Killer. It doesn't make sense."

"But according to our waitress, the prevailing thought in the police department is this suicide-by-extreme-heat idea." Sam looked at her menu, then set it down a second time. "Did Drew tell you any of this? Maybe Drew's seeing this Jen girl but hasn't told his parents because she's a little young for him?"

"I'm sure there are several officers who work at the police department." Rarity decided to try to change the subject before Sam went off on the gruesome guessing game called What Happened to Martha? "Anyway, did you know that Holly works for the police department? Well, really the city, but she's working a project at the station right now, digitizing their records."

"Holly, she's the young, talkative one in your group?" Sam picked up her menu again. "If I was a survivor, I'd join your book club. I haven't had an in-person discussion about books besides what you and I do when I finish one of your recommendations."

Rarity scanned the menu. "Maybe you could be our token healthy person. You know, like a gauge on what's a normal thought process and what's affected by the year or more of treatment?"

"Is that even a thing? I mean, yes, a control group is a thing, but you're not really any different than you were before the cancer, right?"

Jen came back with their iced teas and took their dinner orders, giving Rarity time to think before she answered Sam's question. Which she needed. How did she explain how differently she saw things now? She decided to be truthful, hopefully without a lot of emotion.

After Jen left, Sam leaned forward. "Did I say the wrong thing? You look concerned."

"'Thoughtful' would be a better descriptor, I think." She smiled as she took a sip of the iced tea. "I'm a lot different since before the cancer came into my life. I see most things as a blessing now. And I don't put off things, because you never know what's going to happen in the future. Like getting a dog. I decided and was willing to go and get something as soon as I knew I wanted it in my life. On the other hand, things I used to think were important, like next season's fashions, I don't even look at anymore. After I graduated college, I used to fly to New York for fashion week. Now I really don't care about any of that."

"You are dressing more casual than I've seen you in the past, but I thought that was due to moving to Arizona. You know, 'desert casual'?" Sam nodded. "I thought some of the changes were because we're older now than we were in college. We've both matured, but you have changed from that sorority sister I knew."

"We had fun back then. But do you realize, you're the only sister whom I'm still close to? People kept dropping off year after year, mostly because I stopped going to their fund-raisers. That's when I realized who my real friends were. You miss two fund-raiser invites in a row, and you're off the invite list. But you—you kept calling, and you even came up for a week to hang with me after my surgery." She took a dish and poured some water into it. Then she leaned down and set it on the deck for Killer. "I appreciated that, especially since Kevin had an emergency work trip to the Bahamas that week."

"He did not." Sam's eyes flared. "I mean, I knew he was out of town, but he went to the Caribbean?"

"I didn't find out until he had moved out, a month later. The resort called my number and said I'd left a swimsuit in the villa. I told them to give it to lost and found." Rarity smiled as a server dropped off their dinner entrees. "I felt so much better about our split after that."

"The creep." Sam snapped a picture of her scallop dish. "I wish I'd known. I could have burned all his expensive suits."

"Giving them away to charity was more fun. He hadn't moved everything when I got the call from the resort. By the end of the day, the rest of his stuff was in a Goodwill dumpster waiting to be sorted through. And I stopped answering his calls." Rarity took a bite of her salsa chicken. "This is really good."

"I wish you had told me." Sam touched the top of Rarity's hand to get her attention. "I'm a good listener."

"I just told you. Besides, Kevin moving out was the best thing that's ever happened to me. I didn't have to worry about his feelings about what I was going through. All I needed to do was get better. It made a load of difference in my attitude. He was always either needing to be cheered up about the cancer, or mad at me because I didn't want to go out. It was exhausting." She met Sam's gaze. "I didn't need to add to your worry list. I was fine."

Sam shook her head. "Sometimes you're just a little too independent for your own good. You need to let more people in."

"Which is why I started this book club. And I think you should join. We'll ask the others, but I think they'd like your take on things as well. You're in luck because it looks like we've got an opening."

"Bad joke." Sam laughed anyway.

"Come on Tuesday, and we'll talk to the others." Rarity frowned as her phone rang. "Sorry, it's a transfer from the bookstore number. Let me take this."

Sam moved her hand and picked up her fork. "No problem."

Rarity pushed a button and answered the phone, "The Next Chapter, this is Rarity. Can I help you?"

"Hi, this is Malia. I found Martha's car at a trailhead. I've talked to the others. Do you want to meet us tomorrow at seven at the coffee shop? We're going out there to see if we can find her."

She met Sam's gaze. "Where is the car?"

"I'd go tonight, but Holly's working. The car is unlocked, and it looks like a purse was left in the front seat." Malia paused. "We'll leave right at seven, so if you want coffee, come early."

"Malia, you should call the police," Rarity said, then realized she was talking to dead air. Malia had hung up.

Chapter 6

After talking it out with Sam, Rarity realized she didn't have much, if anything, to call the police about. Malia hadn't told her where the car was, just at a trailhead. There were several around the area. When she'd tried to call Malia back, the person who'd answered the phone told her that it was a public phone at the coffeehouse, but there was no Malia who answered the callout. Sam and Rarity finished their dinner quietly and said good-bye at the corner.

"I'll be at the coffeehouse tomorrow morning to go with you. That way, you have me on your side if you want to try to talk Malia into calling the cops." Sam gave her a quick hug. "But you should leave Killer at home. If we do go hiking, he's not going to like it."

"Yeah, I was already thinking that." Rarity looked down at the little dog who was sitting at her feet. "He probably won't like being left alone, either, but it might get to be too much for him. He doesn't look like much of a hiker."

"You're going to hurt his feelings." Sam laughed and headed down the cross street toward her house.

When Killer and Rarity arrived home, she was beat. She picked up Drew's card and looked at it. On the one hand, she felt like she needed to call and report the new information. On the other, what exactly would she say besides "Be at the coffee shop at seven"? Which would break Malia's trust in her.

She put the card by her keys. She'd take it with her in the morning and make the decision once they found the car. It might not even be Martha's car. Or the cops might have already found it by the time they got there.

She headed to bed with Killer on her heels. She had an early morning.

* * * *

Shirley had a large crossover SUV, and the five of them were crowded inside with coffee and donuts by five after seven the next morning. Kim hadn't come on the adventure because she'd had to work, but she'd asked Shirley to keep her appraised by text as soon as they found anything. If they did.

Rarity glanced at Malia, who was sitting shotgun with a map spread across her lap. "Where are we heading?"

"Devil's Bridge Trailhead. My friend said he saw an abandoned blue Jeep there yesterday afternoon." Malia studied the map closely. "If she went hiking, there's only one trail off there. And maybe we'll get lucky, and she'll have bought a trail pass."

"If she's a hiker, she probably has a senior all-access pass like George and I do." Shirley pointed to her windshield. "It's a lot cheaper than buying a pass every time you want to go hiking."

"Well, that stinks. If she does have one of those, we can't pinpoint when she even came out here." Malia leaned back in her seat. "The hike's only two miles since she parked in the trailhead parking. Can this get up the road, or do we need to park at Dry Creek?"

"I've got four-wheel drive, don't you worry. Besides, I've been up to Devil's Bridge a few times this spring." Shirley sipped her coffee. "Just drink your coffee and relax. We'll be there in about thirty minutes. I felt like a hike this morning, anyway."

"If your friend already hiked the trail, wouldn't he have found"—Rarity paused, not wanting to say 'a body'—"Martha?"

"He didn't see the Jeep until after he came out of the hike. And he only mentioned it to me when we met for coffee last night. He knows I'm looking for one to purchase. I happened to see Martha get in it after the book club, and I was going to talk to her about it on Tuesday, but she never showed. I guess it could be someone else's, but it has an 'I love my Yorkie' sticker on the back window." Malia studied the map.

Rarity was impressed. This was the most she'd ever heard the young woman talk since she'd met her. "I'm glad we're doing this. I wanted to talk to you guys, anyway. Sam was wondering if she could join a book club. Since I only have the one going right now, it's either our group or nothing."

Sam spoke up. "Look, if you don't want me there, I understand. I was just thinking I could bring in a different viewpoint. As a friend of a survivor."

The inside of the crossover was quiet. Finally, Shirley spoke. "We already broke the rules and let Kim in, even though she's not a survivor—yet.

Maybe it would be good to have another member, especially if Martha doesn't come back."

"I don't care either way," Malia chimed in.

Rarity turned to Holly, who was sitting next to her. She was the only one who hadn't spoken her opinion about adding Sam to the group. "What do you think?"

"I liked the idea of it being exclusive. I mean, where can you really talk about chemo and radiation and surgery without people getting weird? But since she's your friend, I'm assuming you two have already had chats like that. So, as long as she's up for our discussions, I agree with Shirley. It might be nice to have a 'rational voice' when we talk." Holly smiled at Sam, who was sitting next to Rarity.

"I'm pretty sure we're all rational," Rarity said as she smiled back at the younger woman.

Holly shook her head. "Not anymore. Having cancer makes you rethink a lot of things. Things that normal people take for granted. Like picking up hiking after a certain age."

"You'd better not be talking about me and George, missy," Shirley called from the front seat, meeting Rarity's gaze in the rearview mirror. Her tone sounded angry, but her eyes were twinkling with humor.

"I'd never talk about you behind your back. Except, of course, when I'm actually behind your back, like I am now, and you can't reach around and swat me without hitting Rarity. And we all know you want Rarity to think you're a nice person." Holly scooted closer to the door and out of Shirley's reach. "You have to realize, I was a kid just a few years ago. I still have my moves."

"Brat." Shirley focused on the road, but Rarity could see the smile. "So, who's finished the first book?"

When they got to the parking lot, Shirley parked as close as she could to the blue Jeep. Then they all got out and studied it. Shirley peeked in the windows. "No one's in the front. And I'm not sure that's a purse. It looks more like a tote."

"Does anyone recognize it as Martha's ride?" Malia glanced at each of the group members in turn. "Okay, then, let's do the hike, and if anyone sees anything unusual, call out, stop, or do something else to get our attention."

"Okay." Rarity couldn't think of anything else to say, so she followed Malia and Holly to the trailhead.

"We'll go first, then Shirley and Sam. Rarity, you bring up the rear." Malia listed off the order for everyone. "And if someone gets tired, just call out 'stop' as well. Then we'll all gather together."

"It's only a two-mile walk. As long as you two aren't jogging, we'll be fine," Shirley pointed out.

"There's a bit of a steep patch at the end." Malia pointed out the hill, then tucked her map into her pocket. "Let's go."

Shirley followed Malia and Holly onto the trailhead, and Sam hurried to catch up. Rarity took one last glace at the parking lot. Besides the Jeep and Shirley's car, there were two other cars parked near the edge of the lot. She took out her phone and took a picture, making sure she got their license plates in the shot.

Then Rarity hurried to follow Sam onto the trail and past the juniper bushes, hoping they wouldn't find Martha, or if they did, that she'd be okay. Maybe she was just hurt, and dehydrated, but not dead. She kept up the mantra. 'Just not dead.' Who said she couldn't be positive and work with the law of attraction?

They didn't find anything on the trail. Holly thought she found a place where it looked like someone had slid down the mountainside, but no one answered when she called Martha's name. When they finally got to Devil's Bridge, Rarity took a breath. It had to be fifty or sixty feet down to the bottom. If Martha had been looking for a place to take herself out, this would be lovely—but not a very nice way to die.

Sam stood next to her. "What do you think?"

"I think we need to call Drew and get him to verify whether that is actually Martha's Jeep in the parking lot. Either way, I think they need to get people down there to see if there's…anything there." Rarity started back down the trail, and the others followed her.

She waited until she was in the car and Shirley was driving them back to Sedona to make the call to the police officer.

He answered on the first ring, his voice gruff with sleep. "Hello?"

Rarity glanced at her watch. It was almost nine. "Sorry, did I wake you?"

"I worked graveyard last night. Who is this? And why am I telling you my life story?"

Rarity could hear a cabinet door open and a cup hit the counter. "Rarity Cole. I have Killer?"

"Oh, sorry, is something wrong with the dog?" Now he sounded alert, worried.

"No, Killer's fine. He's really cute, and he learns really quickly." Rarity saw Sam winding her finger around and around. "Sorry, I'm rambling. Look, we think we found Martha's Jeep out at the Devil's Bridge Trailhead parking lot. You need to send people down to the bridge to make sure she didn't fall over the edge. Or that whoever owns the Jeep didn't fall."

"Okay, this is a lot. One, why are you looking for Martha's car? And two, how did you know it was a Jeep?"

"One of our book club members saw her driving off in it after the first meeting. And it has a Yorkie sticker on the back." Rarity looked at Malia and pushed the phone toward her, but Malia shook her head and pointed back at Rarity. "Anyway, she has a friend who saw it at the trailhead yesterday, so we came up this morning to see if we could find Martha."

"You went to the trailhead to look for Martha?" There was a loud sigh on the other end of the line. "I'm assuming you didn't find her."

Rarity couldn't tell if Drew was angry or just clarifying what she was saying. "Right. We did the full hike and didn't find anything, but the bridge at the end, if someone fell there, well, you know."

"Yes, as a sworn law enforcement agent of the city, I do know. And I'll send someone out to check out the Jeep. If we think, in our professional opinion, there is foul play afoot, we'll call out a search team." He paused, and Rarity could imagine him sipping some of the coffee she was pretty sure he'd made while they were talking. "Is that all? Or do you want to tell me you found Jimmy Hoffa too?"

"Funny. You know, most people don't even know who Jimmy Hoffa is." Rarity was starting to think this had been a bad idea. "Anyway, we just thought you should know."

"Thank you for your interest. I'm sure Martha will be pleased you were worried about her safety."

"Wait, you found her?" Rarity asked.

"Actually, we have a lead on a woman at the Flagstaff hospital. She was found wandering on the road. Our current theory is that someone stole her car and left her out on the road. I'm going up this afternoon to see if it's her."

"Awesome. Just let us know. We are worried about her."

"That's apparent. But you need to let us do our job." He paused again. "I hope you had a nice hike."

"Thanks. I hope that woman is Martha. Maybe Killer will be going back to his home sooner than later."

After she'd hung up, she filled everyone in. "So, maybe Martha's in the hospital."

Malia shook her head. "No way, especially if that was her Jeep. Someone would have taken that to either chop it or sell it out of state. They wouldn't have left it there. Something feels wrong about this whole thing."

"Well, hopefully it was just kids out on a joyride. Maybe Martha was out of the car and hit her head. Then the kids took the car," Shirley theorized.

"Or maybe she's not in the hospital and she's dying somewhere on that mountainside. They need to get out there and look for her." Malia's eyes misted over. "Before it's too late."

The rest of the ride into town was quiet. As soon as they parked in front of the coffee shop, Malia hopped out of the car and headed off down the street.

"I'll go get her. She's worried, that's all." Holly opened her door and hurried after her friend. She caught up with her before Malia turned a corner, and they both disappeared.

"Well, at least we got a good workout this morning." Shirley beamed at Sam and Rarity. "Thanks for coming with us. Those two are fun to be around, but sometimes they have too much energy."

"It was our pleasure. I hope Martha's all right and just in the hospital," Rarity said as she went out the door. "We'll see you on Tuesday."

"With bells on." Shirley's phone buzzed. "There's Kim. She's probably on a break and wants to hear about our adventure. She'll be so excited to hear they might have found Martha."

Sam waved as she shut the back door of Shirley's crossover. She fell in step with Rarity. "Do you want another cup of coffee?"

"Yes, please. That was a weird morning. Malia seems very invested in finding Martha, don't you think?" Rarity held open the door to the coffee shop. "Let's get the coffee to go, and we can walk back to the house so I can get Killer. I hate to have him locked up in the house all day. Especially since it looks like I'll be giving him up soon."

"You don't know that that woman in the hospital is Martha." Sam said as she ordered coffee for the two of them.

"You don't know it's not. And it's the simplest explanation. Why else would she just disappear like that? And really, who would kill her?"

As Rarity walked home to get Killer, she thought about that question. Who would want to kill Martha? She'd been abrupt at the meeting, but all Rarity knew about the woman was that she was widowed, liked Yorkies, had been diagnosed with cancer at some point in her life, and drove a Jeep. She paused at that thought and redialed Drew's number.

"What can I do for you?" He answered the phone with the question.

"Hey, Drew, it's Rarity."

"Yes, I know. I have your phone number in my contacts just in case you need to get in touch with me about Killer. Is everything okay?"

"Well, I was just thinking, maybe we should take Killer out to see the Jeep. He might be able to tell us that it's Martha's." She waited for his answer.

"You mean, like bark and want to get inside?" Drew asked, then continued without letting her answer. "Because I don't really speak dog. Do you?"

"No, I guess it wasn't that good of an idea. I just thought that if Killer recognized it, you might be able to use that recognition to get a search party out there to look for Martha. It's already been a few days." Rarity paused at her mailbox and resisted the idea of opening it until she finished the conversation. Besides, it was probably still empty. But mail came early here so the carriers could get in and out of the weather.

"I don't know about using the dog. I was going to look up the plates and see whom the vehicle is registered to. What do you think about that? Maybe it will work?"

"You're teasing me. Okay, I didn't think about you being able to look up plates." She opened the mailbox anyway. Bill, bill, and a flyer for a community picnic next week. "Sorry to have bothered you."

"It's not a bother, but Rarity? You need to stay out of investigating things. One, we don't know whether Martha's safe or not." He turned down the stereo in his car. "Hopefully, this woman in the hospital is her and she just has a slight memory problem. Then you'll lose your new roommate."

"Yes, that would be the best outcome," Rarity agreed. She sighed and focused on the call. "Sorry to bother you."

"No worries. I'm not even in town yet. Killer's doing good?"

Rarity spent the next ten minutes telling him about the cute tricks the dog knew and the way the dog would watch her doing her daily routines. She startled when she heard Killer barking from inside. "Look, I've got to go. Thanks for being so open-minded about this whole thing."

"I'll call you and give you a warning if this is Martha. You're probably going to have to go into cute puppy detox as soon as she comes and gets the dog."

After he hung up, she wondered if he wasn't right. She loaded Killer's things into her bag, leaving the second collar at home. She didn't know if it was for walking or what, but the thing was so heavy, she didn't want him to have to deal with that and the walk, especially with it being hotter than he was used to when they went to the shop.

She was definitely going to have to go through detox, because she was in love with this little dog.

Chapter 7

She didn't hear from Drew that night, but as soon as the shop opened Saturday morning, both Holly and Malia were sitting on her couch, waiting for her to finish with a customer. Killer was perched between them, so when one stopped petting him to talk, the other one would pick up the slack. The dog had skills.

When there were no other customers, Rarity came back to the fireplace and sat down. "What are you two doing up so early?"

"I found something at the police station about Martha. Her husband didn't die—he ran off with Madame Zelda's husband, Charles, ten years ago. They said they were going to work in the North Dakota oil fields, but they never reported to work. They just vanished." Holly made a *poof* motion with her hands and then let them fall apart. "Now Martha's missing. What do you want to bet that Madame Zelda was the one who did her in? She's always talking about the spirit world. Maybe she knows so many of them because she's killed so many people?"

Rarity checked Holly's body language. The girl actually thought the fortune-teller could have been involved. "Look, let's not turn this into a witch hunt just because Madame Zelda knew the victim. Maybe one of us should go get a reading and see what she says."

Holly nodded like Rarity had suggested she walk on hot coals. "I don't think I could do it, though. My folks, well, they were pretty strict, so I'm not comfortable with opening myself up to the other side. Besides, if the police department knew I was talking about the old records, I could get in trouble."

"Cold cases are open to everyone with a request." Malia pulled out her phone and made a note. "I'll ask about the case Monday morning. I can say someone said something about it in passing and I was interested. And I can't do a reading because I just got one last month. I do one every other month. If I change my routine, she'll be suspicious."

Rarity leaned back in her chair. "I guess I'm getting a reading, then. Her shop is open later than mine. I can see if I can get one tonight."

"Call and see if she has openings. She's very popular." Malia opened her contact section and rattled off a number. "Make sure you ask for a first-timer's discount when you call. I think she shortens your time a bit, but it will save you fifty percent."

"Okay, then." Rarity pulled out her cell phone and made the call. A young girl informed her that Madame Zelda wouldn't be available until Monday night at six thirty. Rarity took the appointment and then hung up. She made note of it on her paper planner. "I guess I'm getting my tea leaves read."

Malia shook her head. "No one does that anymore. Madame Zelda uses tarot cards."

"And you'll both be able to report on what you find out during our book club meeting." Holly stood and pulled Malia to her feet. "We've got a mani-pedi appointment in Flagstaff but wanted to get you up-to-date, especially since your store is right next door to hers. I hate to see you get hurt."

Rarity was busy with the store right up to closing. When the bell rang as she was clearing the cash register, she called out, "Sorry, we're closing up."

Killer started barking his happy bark and ran to the door.

"Make sure that door's closed," Rarity called out as she looked up to see Drew leaning down to pick up the little dog.

"I got it." He turned and jiggled it. "I'm going to lock it and turn your sign to *Closed* if you don't mind. I need to talk to you."

Rarity's heart sank. They'd found Martha, and Drew was here to pick up Killer. She swallowed away the pain. How could a dog get so into her heart in just a few days? "Not a problem. Come over here, and we can talk while I close up the register. Do you want coffee? I made it around three, so it's pretty dark."

"Actually, that would be awesome. Black is fine. I've got to go back to the office anyway, and this will help me stay awake while I'm working." He leaned against the counter.

"Lots of paperwork in a missing persons case, I guess." She turned away and poured the coffee into a large disposable cup. She grabbed a bottle of water for herself.

"More with a murder case." He took the coffee from her.

His words took a while to sink in. She avoided looking over to the fireplace area where Martha had sat during the book club. Her chest hurt a bit as she formed the words. "Wait, Martha was murdered? Was that her Jeep?"

He nodded. "It was. I think whoever killed her thought if we found the Jeep there, we'd assume she was hiking and fell. We found her body at the bottom of the hill just off the trail by the bridge. The evidence doesn't point to a fall. She was hit in the head with what appears to be a tire iron."

Rarity covered her mouth. "Oh my God. When did she die? Who would have killed her?"

Killer was watching her and whimpered a bit at her show of emotion. Drew rubbed his ears. "The coroner will figure the how and when. But as far as who and why, we have no clue. Yet."

She opened her water and took a sip. "Wow. I mean, I knew people who died. Older relatives, people who were in treatment with me. But you could see the toll the treatments were taking. And Martha wasn't that old."

"Fifty-six. And she'd been starting to date a man at her church. At least that's what my mom told me when we found out she was missing. Now, even that relationship is going to be looked at with a fine-tooth comb." He sipped his coffee. "Anyway, I guess I wanted to tell you that keeping Killer isn't just a temporary thing anymore. If you want, I'll start looking for a permanent home for him."

"No!" It came out harder and faster than even she'd imagined. She waved a hand in apology. "Actually, I've been worried that you were coming to take him away from me. He's become part of the family way too fast. Maybe he had a premonition that his owner wasn't coming home and he needed to settle into a new family?"

He nodded, giving the dog a kiss on the head. "He seems like a smart dog. Like I said, I would have kept him if my folks weren't staying with me."

When he stood, he put Killer on the floor.

"I guess you have to get back?" She reached over and took his cup. "If you don't hate it, you can have the rest of the pot, or I can dump this."

"Give me the rest." He smiled, and Rarity noticed he had a dimple in his left cheek.

Stupid thing to notice, she thought as she turned to set up his coffee. She put a top on the cup. "Here you go. Don't work too late."

"That's your job when you're the only detective in the station." He held up the cup. "Thank you for this. Do you want me to drive you home?"

"No, I'll be fine. I'll be out of here in less than five minutes, then the walkway is all lit up." She smiled over at the dog, who'd returned to his bed by the fireplace. He had a stuffed animal and was chewing on its ear. "Besides, I have Killer."

"Which makes me ask again, do you want a ride?" He held his hands up and laughed when she gasped at his insinuation. "Anyway, be safe. I don't think there's a crazed serial killer out there, but it's just my luck if I tell you there's not and there is one."

"I won't hold you to it or haunt you if I get killed." She put her tote on her shoulder. "I can't speak for Killer, however."

"You're funny." He didn't leave the store.

She put Killer's leash on and picked up his toys. The store would be closed tomorrow. Most of Sedona was closed on Sundays unless there was a festival, but this was an off weekend, so she had big laundry and reading plans. "Thanks for letting me know."

He held the door open and then waited as she locked it and set the alarm. He paused at the sidewalk. "I'm glad you get to keep him."

She watched as he got into his truck and drove away. There were still a lot of people on the streets. Probably walking to and from the restaurants. Before she'd come in to open the shop that day, Rarity had taken chicken out of the freezer to thaw. She might have a glass of wine with dinner. This time to celebrate her newest family member, Killer. And to mourn the loss of his last owner, Martha. A woman she hadn't had time to get to know at all.

The rumor mill was late getting the memo about Martha, and she didn't get any calls from the book club members until Sunday night. She should have called them, but it still didn't feel real. She wanted to process the idea herself so she wouldn't be a crying mess when she called. She'd spent the day getting ready for her next week, as well as just hanging out with her new dog.

Ignoring the feelings she had around Martha's death. Staying busy had always been the way she dealt with unsettling news.

And she had a lot of distractions to fall back on. She needed to take Killer to the vet, but she'd rather see if Martha had used someone specifically. Calling Flagstaff vets had gone on her Monday to-do list. Along with figuring out if she needed to tag the dog. Some areas did. Others ignored the idea, even though having a tag increased the number of pet returns when they ran off. Either way, she was getting him the shot, for her piece of mind.

Sam was the first to call.

"Hey, are you okay?" Sam's voice sounded breathless as she checked in.

Rarity set the book down she'd been reading. "I'm fine. I guess you heard about Martha."

"Shirley came into my shop this morning and told me. I didn't really know Martha, but it's a shock that someone was killed, right here in Sedona."

"Maybe we can get a collection going to send flowers to the funeral." Rarity pulled her planner over and put a note in about flowers and the funeral. "I wonder if I should go and take Killer? Do dogs go to funerals?"

"Do you think we should stop looking into this? I think Shirley's been in the library all weekend looking at old newspapers." Sam paused before she asked, "Don't you want to know who killed her?"

"I think that's Drew's job, he's in law enforcement. Not us." Rarity looked over at Killer, who was lying on the couch watching her. He whined softly.

"Okay, but you need to tell your group. I'm not telling them that the Choose Your Own Adventure part of the club has been cancelled," Sam said. "See you Monday."

"Yeah." Rarity disconnected the call and put her phone down. Killer was still watching her. "We're not real investigators. All we're going to do is mess things up."

Killer lay his head down between his feet but kept watching her. He whined again.

"Seriously? You want us to find out who killed Martha?"

Killer stood up and barked twice. His entire body shook with the bark.

Rarity stood and walked over to the couch. She picked him up and rubbed underneath his chin. "Okay, I'll go get my fortune told tomorrow night. That's all I agreed to. Besides, Drew will probably have this entire case solved before I can even do that."

Killer leaned his head into her chest as if he was telling her that he had faith in his new owner. Rarity walked outside and sat on the deck watching the night sky. She didn't have faith in her ability, not one bit.

* * * *

Monday went by slowly, but when it was time for her reading, Shirley showed up at the bookstore. "What are you doing here?"

"Well, I figured I could watch the shop. Maybe keep people here until you get back, or I could probably figure out the cash register if someone wanted to buy something." She looked at the machine with a touch of fear in her eyes. "Either way, you need someone to watch Killer."

"That's true. I don't want to take him inside. Especially if Madame Zelda actually did know Martha. She'd know her dog, too, right?" Rarity went through a quick how-to on selling a book. She canceled out the fake sale she'd done to show Shirley and smiled. "Easy-peasy, right?"

"I might just tell them you'll be back in a few minutes." Shirley smiled, but her face was a little green. "Can you show me one more time?"

Rarity went through the register process again, this time a little slower. Then she glanced at the clock. "I've got to go. If you're not comfortable, just tell them I'll be back at seven. The receptionist said my first visit would only last thirty minutes."

"Unless she knocks you unconscious because you've figured out her evil plan." Shirley pulled her book out of her tote and settled in. "I really hope we have time tomorrow to talk about this. I am loving it."

"I'm sure we will." Rarity slipped her cross tote over one shoulder. "I loved the book, too."

And with that, she left the shop and went next door. The outer room smelled of some sort of spice and wax. Candles were lit all over the small display room. A curtain was on the left wall, and when she went in, a bell rang. Madame Zelda floated out from behind the curtain and stopped when she saw Rarity standing there.

"You're my six thirty?"

Rarity nodded, shifting back and forth on her feet. "Yep. I've never had a reading before so I thought it was time."

Madame Zelda narrowed her eyes and took in Rarity's posture. "Well, let's get it over with, then. I've got a dinner date at seven thirty."

"Oh? Are you seeing someone?" Rarity followed Madame Zelda into a small room. It had been painted black and had silver stars all over the top of the room. She sat in the only other chair after Madame Zelda took her place. The small table held tarot cards and one of those large glass balls.

"My love life is none of your concern." She held her hands outstretched and palms up on the table. "Relax and put your hands in mine."

Rarity adjusted her crossbody tote and then laid her hands on the other woman's. "I thought we'd do cards."

"We will, but I want to connect with your aura first." She paused, then frowned. "You have had many changes recently. Some I knew about, but you have a new roommate?"

"How did you know?" Rarity was beginning to freak out a bit.

The woman cracked a smile. "Madame Zelda never reveals her secrets, but I did see you walking Martha's dog last week. I'm glad Killer had a place to go. Martha's passing has been upsetting."

"Oh, you knew her?" Rarity asked.

Madame Zelda pulled her hands back and somehow pushed Rarity's away with the same movement. "We are here to find out about you. I want you to get your money's worth."

"Thanks, that's kind." Rarity leaned in as Madame Zelda shuffled the cards. She pushed the pile toward Rarity. "Cut."

"Excuse me?"

Madame Zelda sighed. "Cut the cards. Like when you're playing a game?"

"Oh yeah." Rarity reached out and cut the cards, then again at Madame Zelda's instruction. When she did it a third time, Rarity wondered if this was a stalling tactic, but then Madame Zelda started laying the cards out on the table. Eleven cards, all with brightly colored pictures on the front.

Rarity looked down on the three that Madam Zelda pushed toward her.

"Your past, your present, and your future." She tapped each card with the time frame it represented. She touched the first card, which displayed a woman with seven wands. "You were challenged and won—you persevered through some bad times. I'm assuming the cards have picked up on your cancer diagnosis."

"Yes, I'd say that was spot-on." Rarity stared at the card, wondering how hard it would have been for Madame Zelda to make sure that card showed up in her reading.

"You still doubt me. No matter." Madame Zelda pulled a second card, the three of cups. On it, women were dancing together. "Your book club is made up of true friends. Maybe not yet, but they'll get there. Women taking care of each other. I've always loved this card. It speaks of celebrations and collaborations."

"You think it's referring to my book club?" Rarity looked at her, understanding now what had happened. "Did you give my flyer to Martha?"

"I've told you I don't gossip about my clients, but since she's passed on, I guess she's not technically my client anymore. Yes, the flyer went to Martha. I was hoping she'd open up with others who had gone through the same thing. She held so much pain and anger inside. Why else would she name that sweet little dog, Killer?" She turned over the third card. It was the Death card. "Endings, change, transitions."

"Martha seemed not to be able to let go of the past. Is that what your cards are saying? Ending because of the inability to let go of the past." Rarity could see it. Having cancer for some people was like a badge of honor. It was the most important thing about their lives—before and after.

Madame Zelda met her gaze. "Dear, these aren't Martha's cards. They're yours. You have an ending coming soon if you're not careful."

Chapter 8

Tuesday night the group was at the bookstore fifteen minutes before the start of the book club. They all gathered around the fireplace and set their books on the table. Shirley had brought Texas sheet cake for the group, and she was busy cutting slices for everyone.

Holly was midstory. "It was my third chemo treatment, and the first two hadn't bothered me—to the point I was wondering if I'd even lose my hair. I'd read somewhere that some people don't. Anyway, the nurse was kind and tried to let me down easy. A guy in the treatment pod spoke up and said he hadn't lost his hair until the second chemo. He'd been getting ready to shave and had put on shaving cream. All of his hair came off with the cream. He didn't even have to pick up a razor. Of course, my hair fell out the next week. Thank goodness I'd bought a wig after the first treatment, just in case."

Rarity put up the sign by the door and then joined the group by the fireplace. After a few more hair loss stories, they settled in, and Shirley spoke up. "I found some things about Martha and her husband in the library."

Kim choked on the coffee she'd just taken a sip of. She set the cup on the table and wiped her face with a napkin. "Don't tell me you went snooping?"

"Hold on before you answer that. We need to make a decision before we go any further. We're supposed to be a book club. For people who have been touched by cancer or have had friends go through treatment. Like Sam. But with Martha's death, I think we're turning into something more. And I think we need to discuss this before it goes any further. Maybe some of us, like Kim, just want to be here for the book discussions." Rarity looked around at the members.

"I didn't mean that. I feel as badly about Martha as the rest of you, but investigations should be left to the professionals, don't you think?" Kim looked around at the other four, and from their expressions, Rarity saw the answer. And so did Kim.

Rarity took a deep breath. "Okay, so we're now a book club and murder-investigating group? What can we even find out?"

"There's a lot," Holly said, glancing at Malia. "We found her car—the police didn't. We pointed them in the right direction to find her body. And now that we have evidence of her connection with Madame Zelda, we might have found her killer."

"The fortune teller? You think *she* killed Martha?" Kim leaned back in her chair. "This is getting interesting."

"Okay, I guess the vote is done. Everyone wants to go down this path?" Rarity met each member's gaze and waited for them to nod. Even Sam agreed. "Then the Tuesday Night Survivors' Club just turned into the Tuesday Night Sleuthers' Club."

"It has a nice ring to it." Sam smiled at her. "Bonus, I get a full membership card instead of just an associate member."

The group laughed, and Shirley handed everyone a three-ring binder.

Rarity met puzzled gazes around the group. "Shirley, what's this?"

"It's a notebook where we can all write down the clues and add to it when we find out more." Shirley looked at Rarity like she'd grown a second head.

"Of course it is." Rarity opened the book. Sometimes she felt like the book club was getting away from her. Other times—like this—she was certain.

Shirley took her comment as approval. "Okay, so I've put paper in this, lined and blank, so we can make notes and draw out maps if we need to. I made a report of what I found in the library and added a report on what 'someone who shall not be named' found out about Madame Zelda's family and Martha's."

"During my reading, she admitted that Martha was one of her clients. And that she'd given her the flyer to try to get her to attend the book club." Rarity glanced through the notes. "That doesn't seem like someone who wanted Martha dead."

"Maybe they got in a fight about something else," Malia offered. "Typically, it's love or money."

"Did either woman have money?" Rarity asked the group. Everyone just shrugged. "I know both Martha and Madame Zelda are—were—dating someone. Drew told me that Martha was seeing someone. And Madame Zelda had a date after my reading last night."

Holly held up a hand. "I saw her going into the Garnet last night. I grabbed some takeout to eat at my desk, and she was coming in when I was going out. I didn't see who she met, though."

"So, that's the next assignment. Who is Madame Zelda seeing, and who was Martha seeing?" Shirley ate a bite of her cake. "Wouldn't it be fun if it was the same man? If they had a fight over a guy?"

"That would be horrible." Malia shook her head. "I don't know why everything has to be about some guy and how they did the women in their lives wrong. Aren't there any good guys left in the world?"

"One can only hope," Sam said.

"Oh dear, I offended you. I am so sorry. Sometimes I speak before I think. It's just that in my day, we did a lot for our significant others." Shirley looked around the group. "Can you forgive me?"

"Shirley, you're fine. We all have different viewpoints and come from different places." Rarity looked around the group. "We need to be sensitive to other people's feelings when we speak, but we should also assume we all have the best of intentions when we do."

"My mom used to tell us to use three questions as your guide. Is it true? Is it kind? And is it helpful?" Holly added to the discussion.

"I didn't mean to imply that you were wrong in what you said." Malia went over and gave Shirley a hug.

"Besides, there are no bad ideas in brainstorming, right?" Sam said, looking around the room.

Kim shrugged. "Sometimes there are really bad ideas during a brainstorming session. And the sooner you acknowledge that, the better."

Kim's words echoed in the group. Rarity could see the effect they had on the others. Where the other women had been trying to ease Shirley's pain, Kim seemed to want to add to it.

Rarity held up a hand. "So, we have a couple of questions about these mystery men. Anyone want to take the lead on finding out who Martha was seeing?"

"I could call Drew and see if he knows," Sam offered.

"But why would he tell you?" Holly pointed to Rarity. "She has Martha's dog. Maybe Rarity could get into Martha's house and find her address book. She seemed like the type to have a paper list of numbers and names."

"Drew said Martha had a datebook. Maybe he'd let me look through it to find out when Killer's last vet appointment was and whom she took him to. It might also have names and numbers of her contacts and friends." Rarity shot an apologetic look at Sam. "I'll go over tomorrow morning to the station and see if he has the datebook. Getting Killer's vet's name has been on my list for days anyway."

"I'll come with you," Sam added. "I can distract him while you go through the book."

Rarity wrote a note down in her planner that she had next to her. She'd brought it over to mark the next book they were going to read so she could buy copies, but noting her investigating duties worked too. "So, who's finding out more about Madame Zelda's date?"

Holly raised her hand. "I'm friends with the bartender over at the Garnet. He's super nice. And I know he was there because I chatted with him before my takeout was ready. He should know who Madame Zelda met there. It's not that big of a place."

"I think you all are taking this a little too far, but whatever. It's fun to watch you." Kim tucked her book into her purse. "So are we starting a new book next week?"

"I thought maybe we'd take a week off, so we can talk about this book next week. You all need to send me some recommendations this week. Or write them down and leave them on the counter. I'll pick two choices, and we'll make the decision next week." Rarity looked around the room. It was almost nine. The time had flown. "Anything else to discuss?"

Malia raised her hand. "I'm going to talk to my friend and see if he can pinpoint how long Martha's car was out there. He's a ranger, so he visits all of the trailheads and has access to the security feed."

"You don't think he'll rat you out to Drew, will he?" Rarity thought about how Drew had told her that this wasn't her investigation.

"I don't think so." Malia glanced at Shirley and sighed. "Okay, so we've dated a few times, and he likes me. Don't read anything into that."

Shirley started giggling first, then the rest of the group joined in. Malia's face turned red and then she started laughing too. "Okay, fine, he likes me. I'm just not sure if I'm ready to start dating yet."

The rest of the meeting was spent talking about dating and the pros and cons. They might not be reading romance, Rarity thought, but the subject had still wormed its way into their discussions.

After the others had left, Sam picked up the last copy of the book that they were discussing next week. "I guess I'd better read this if I'm going to be part of the group."

"I figured you hadn't, which is why I stalled Kim." Rarity rang up the sale and gave Sam the friendship discount. "She was a little harsh tonight, don't you think?"

"Maybe she got some bad news this week." Sam picked Killer up and rubbed his belly. "Isn't she the one still going through treatment?"

Rarity nodded as she ran Sam's credit card. "Yeah, but she was almost mean to Shirley. And Shirley's the one who brought her into the group. Maybe I should have a talk with Kim about watching her words during the meeting."

"Do you have any information about her? Where she works? If it's local, you could go visit and take her for coffee. That way you're not doing it before or after a meeting. Kind of neutral ground." Sam tucked the bag in her purse. "I'll walk with you to my corner if you don't take too long closing up."

"All I have to do is look up Kim's address and then turn off the lights." She pulled out a folder where she kept all the information about the book club. She flipped through the intro page each member had turned in at the first meeting they'd attended. Kim's page was almost empty. She read it aloud to Sam. "This is weird. Listen. Kim Smith, age twenty-eight, going through chemo and radiation now at Flagstaff Cancer Center. Occupation, lawyer."

"That's it?" Sam took the page from Rarity. "She didn't fill in anything about her favorite reads, how far away she lives, emergency contact. And if she's twenty-eight, so am I."

"Yeah, I would have pegged her for being in her late thirties. Maybe she meant to say thirty-eight?" Rarity took the page back and put it away in her file. "Or she lied on the form. Gave us bogus information because she didn't think I needed to know that about her. I'm sure Martha left a lot empty too."

"Let's see." Sam nodded to the folder.

Rarity pulled Martha's questionnaire out. It listed off everything Rarity had asked, including an emergency contact. She tapped her finger on it. "Eric Redding. Her son?"

"Probably." Sam wrote down the name and phone number on a piece of paper. "Now I have something to talk to Drew about. Maybe he didn't know about this emergency contact?"

"Maybe." Rarity thought maybe Drew would wonder why Rarity hadn't asked him about it, but she figured Sam would improvise if, or when, Drew asked her how she got the information. Which would give her more time with Martha's planner.

* * * *

Wednesday morning, Rarity and Sam were at the police station right at eight. They ran into Drew and his parents when they were coming out the front door. Rarity glanced at Sam. "Hey, Drew, I wanted to stop by and see if I could go through Martha's planner. I need to find Killer's vet."

"Sam, how are you, dear?" Edith Anderson pulled Sam into a bear hug. "Drew, this is Sam, the young woman I've been telling you about."

"Nice to meet you, Sam." Drew nodded, then pulled Rarity aside. "Can it wait? We're heading to breakfast. They want to tell me something."

"Drew, maybe Sam and her friend want to come to breakfast with us?" Edith called over to where he and Rarity were talking.

He sighed and shook his head. "So much for them telling me about finding the perfect house to move into."

Rarity giggled, and they stepped back toward the group. "Actually, I can't go to breakfast. I've got to open the bookstore soon. I was hoping that Martha's planner had information about where she took Killer and when his shots were due. I tried to call a few of the veterinarians, but the front staff was less than helpful and told me they'd call me back. Surprisingly, I haven't heard from anyone."

He nodded. "We've gone over it for any clues and haven't found anything, so I can let you look. If you wear gloves and sit in my office to read it."

"I can do that. I've got a little time before I have to open the store. Sam, why don't you go with Drew and his folks. You were just saying you were hungry." Rarity nodded toward the station door. "Where will I find it?"

"Hold on a minute." Drew turned to his folks. "Mom, Dad, why don't you and your friend go along to the restaurant. I'll be there as soon as I set up Rarity in my office. It shouldn't take more than ten, fifteen minutes at most."

"Probably five," Rarity added for Sam's benefit. She knew her friend liked the Andersons, but what she really wanted was some time with Drew to see if they were compatible at all.

Jonathon took his wife's arm and offered the other one to Sam. "We'll see you at the restaurant, son. Don't hurry on my account. I'll enjoy having a meal with two lovely ladies."

Drew put his hand on Rarity's shoulder and turned her toward the station. "Let's find you that book. Then I guess I'll go have breakfast with your friend since my folks are bound and determined to find me a wife. Maybe if I started dating they'd move out of my house to give me some privacy."

"One could only hope." Rarity walked into the station with him. For a police station, it was kind of friendly-looking. A woman sat at a counter at the end of the room, but there were couches and a fireplace on the other wall.

Drew must have seen her pause to look around the waiting room. "We have community meetings here sometimes at night. It's a safe place, and we just lock the front door once everyone's here. We have a couple of AA meetings and other support groups that use it. You wouldn't believe the number of charlatans who come to meetings like this to promote their rehab or their miracle cure. It slows them down a bit if the meetings are held at a police station. Hopefully, you won't have that with your cancer group."

"I'd never thought it might even be an issue before now." She followed him into the hallway. "We're a small group, so if someone did try to sell snake oil, I think we'd see it."

"Well, just keep in mind, not everyone's up-front with what they say they want." He opened a door and nodded. "This is my office."

Rarity felt her face heat up as she thought about her ulterior motive for wanting to see Martha's planner. He couldn't be thinking she was lying, could he? The office was sterile, with one desk, one office chair, and two plastic visitor's chairs. If the lobby said *welcome, stay a while*, this room screamed, *get out now, I'm busy*. "It's"—she searched for a word—"practical."

Drew laughed and pointed for her to sit in his chair. "That is why I like you, Rarity. You're unfailingly kind. My mom just said I needed at least one thing that was personal in the office. So, I'm thinking she'll show up tomorrow with pillows and framed pictures of my college, high school, and kindergarten graduation ceremonies. As well as my Eagle Scout ceremony."

"Could be worse." She took a seat at the desk as he handed her a pair of gloves.

"Explain?" He took the journal out of the bottom drawer and opened it, using the edge of the plastic bag it had come out of.

"It could be old prom pictures. Especially if the young lady was still in town and still single." She slipped on the gloves and took out her journal and a pen. She set them next to the planner. "Just in case I get lucky."

"Okay, so you're right, that would be way worse. Hopefully, she doesn't think of that." He pointed to the reception area, where Rarity could see the woman they'd seen when they'd first come inside. "Just leave the book here when you're done and close the door. Let Sue know that you're leaving. I'll tell her you're in here, so you don't scare her when you leave. It can get kind of quiet in here when everyone's out on calls."

"Have a fun breakfast." Rarity opened the journal and started to page through it, hoping to find a list of doctors, dentists, and other professionals who Martha used. When Rarity had gone through her treatments, she'd seen so many people, she'd made a little book that listed all the doctors, addresses, phone numbers, appointment times, and who referred her. It seemed overwhelming at times, but she knew she was organized, so that helped with her anxiety.

"Are you sure you don't need help?" He held his hands out. "I'm begging you, please help keep me away from another blind date with my parents tagging along."

"Seriously, Sam's a good egg. You'll like her. Your parents like her, so that's a good sign, right?" She met his gaze, setting her pen down.

"You should have seen the last girl they liked. I wasn't sure I hadn't seen her on the newest FBI Most Wanted sheets we get faxed every week." He tapped the chair he was standing next to with two fingers, a habit she'd seen him do a couple of times. "Well, call me if you need me or find something I didn't notice."

"You think I might find a clue?" Now Rarity felt like a fool, trying to hide what she was actually looking for.

"I doubt it, but a second set of eyes never hurts." He waved as he walked out the door. "Tell Killer I said hi."

Rarity watched as he disappeared out the door and down the hallway. She heard him call out to the receptionist and then heard a door shut. Besides the faint hum of a radio, which must be at the receptionist's desk, the place was quiet. Too quiet. The bookstore never really got this way since it had businesses on both sides of it. If it wasn't noise from the street, she could hear the pipes and air conditioners in her building.

She returned to her job, finding Killer's vet and determining when his last appointment was. And, if she was lucky, the name and phone number of Martha's new beau. Drew had probably already talked to him, but like he'd said, another set of eyes.

She shook her head, wondering how she'd gotten herself talked into this plan. Her new motto of taking risks seemed to be having unintended consequences. Like lying to the local police.

Chapter 9

Rarity was back at the bookstore with Killer when Sam came in from her breakfast. She set the notebook aside and put down her pen. "So how did breakfast go?"

Sam shrugged. "Okay, I guess. Drew wasn't very talkative, and his folks kept talking him up, which made him totally embarrassed. I've never seen anyone so red. Did you know he was an Eagle Scout?"

"Actually, yes. He mentioned it today when he was setting me up in his office to read Martha's journal. I think you should give him some space. His folks do this a lot. If you're interested in him, maybe you should try to develop a friendship first, with no strings."

"Like you have?" Sam leaned on the counter. "You'd tell me if you were interested in him, right?"

"If I was interested in him as more than a friend, yes, I'd tell you. Drew and I just have Killer in common. He's a nice guy, but right now, I'm not sure I trust my judgment with any guy. I don't have the best track record."

"You can't blame yourself for Kevin. He put up a good front. I was even entranced for a while, until I heard the way he treated you during your treatments." Sam squeezed her arm. "You're a catch. And if he couldn't see that, he's a jerk."

"Then he's definitely a jerk." Rarity didn't want to talk about Kevin and the things he'd said and done during her treatments. She was just glad to know who he truly was before she'd said yes and had to undo all the ways two people's lives mixed together when they got married. "Anyway, sorry the breakfast wasn't what you or he expected. I did find some things in the datebook, though."

"Like what?" Sam reacted.

"Like a vet for Killer and his next appointment. I've already called, and they said I can just keep the same time and they'll switch his file over to me when I get there." Rarity grinned. "One problem solved."

"I was actually asking about Martha's death. But that's exciting too." Sam glanced at her watch.

"I also made a list of several men who were mentioned in Martha's journal. She didn't put anyone's name next to the Date Night entries she had once or twice a month, so we have a list of five." Rarity passed the list to Sam, who used her finger as she glanced down the list. "Does anyone look familiar?"

"I know a Roger, but he's married and he's a plumber, so maybe he's not the same one? I know several Keiths, but no Kellys or Tims." She pointed to the last name on the list. "Robert is a common name around here, but there's a minister by that name. Do we know what church, if any, Martha went to?"

"She went to church. It was in her planner, and she took cookies for the second service last week." Rarity tried to remember if the name of the church had been mentioned. "I don't know where she went, sorry."

"Well, it's something. And maybe Shirley would know more. She's been around for years and seems to know everyone." Sam headed to the door. "I need to get going."

"See you. And don't say that to Shirley, she might think you're saying she's old."

Killer whined as Sam disappeared out the door and then went to stand by the window next to it, watching Sam until she got swallowed up in the crowd. Then he came back to his bed by the fireplace. It was time for his midday nap. And Rarity had work to do as well. Work that wasn't all about finding out what happened to Martha.

The rest of the day went by slowly. She probably had seven customers come in the bookstore. She knew Wednesdays might be the slow day from things other business owners had said, so she wasn't really worried. Yet. The bell over the door went off just as she was thinking about closing early and heading home for a swim.

The hiking instructor walked into the bookstore. Ender, no, that wasn't his first name, it was something else...Archer. That was it. She ran a hand over her curly hair and then shoved it under the counter. What was she doing? She smiled and nodded, deciding not to call him by name, just in case she was wrong. "Good afternoon. Nice to see you again."

He came over to the counter and leaned on it. His dark hair curled over his ears, and his tan made him look like he should be surfing, not hanging out in a bookstore. He held out his hand, "Archer Enders. I'm glad that you remembered me, I wasn't sure you would."

"It was a lovely tour. I've never seen anything quite like the area. I need to get out exploring more, but I've been tied to setting up the bookstore." She smiled softly, hoping he didn't think she was just hiding.

"You should come to the Saturday tour. We're going to Munds Wagon Trail. It has a lot of history as well as beautiful scenery. You should be back in time to open." His smile was easy and infectious.

"I'll have to see if my friend is available." She wrote a note on a piece of paper. "I'd love to come."

"I'll save you two spots on the bus. As long as this friend is female." He held her gaze with his, and Rarity realized his eyes were a stunning blue gray. "I'm sorry, that was forward of me. I'll hold two spots and hope you come."

"I'll check with her later, and we'll give you a call." She wondered why it was suddenly so hot in the store. Maybe she needed to get the air conditioner fixed.

"I've been thinking of you since I met you." He laughed. "I shouldn't have said that and showed my cards. Anyway, on a more professional note, what books do you have on hiking in the area? You mentioned you might want to stock some that I could refer people to if they couldn't fit in my tours." He took out a notebook and a pen.

"Let's go see. I have an entire shelf of Sedona-related books available. You can tell me what I'm missing and what I need to stock up with." She stepped around the counter, thankful for a change of subject. He'd been flirting with her. And since that hadn't happened to her in years, she hadn't been prepared for it.

They talked books, which was a much safer subject for Rarity, but when his fingers brushed hers accidentally, she felt the jolt. She pushed the emotion away and turned toward her computer, where they'd been looking up the availability of the books from a list he'd brought.

"I think I can order these three and get them at a price point your customers will appreciate. The other two, they're out of print, so I would be buying them from a secondhand seller. I can see if I can get a few, but they're going to be pricey." She wrote some prices on the sheet and handed it back to him. "I'll order ten of each, and we'll see how it goes."

"Perfect. I'll write up a sheet to put in the office for when people show up. Do you have a logo you can send me or any header information?" He tucked the note into his shirt pocket.

"I do. I'll send it over, and you can add it. Marketing was my job before I decided to quit the easy life and open my own business."

He laughed. "Same here. I was a corporate lawyer. The pay was great, but the scenery was horrible. Even on the fifteenth floor. Not like here."

"Are you new to the area?" She glanced at her watch. Time to start closing up.

"Yeah. I've been here about three years, which means I'm still a newcomer to the old guys." He stood and glanced out the window. "I guess you need to close up."

"Yeah, Killer and I need to get home. It's his dinnertime."

He frowned and looked around the bookstore. "Killer?"

Rarity walked over to the fireplace and picked up the little dog from his bed, where he'd been still sleeping. She ruffled his hair. "Some guard dog you are."

"I didn't see him." Archer held his hand out for Killer to sniff. "May I pet him?"

"Of course, if he'll let you. I haven't seen him not like anyone yet." Rarity watched as Archer leaned in and stroked the dog's fur.

"Aren't you a special little one?" He smiled and nodded. "I'll see you Saturday, maybe?"

"Probably. Seven again?"

"Yep. Bring your coffee. The lines at the coffee shop can get a little long on Saturday mornings before the hikes take off." He tipped his hat and started to leave when a book caught his eye. "Sorry, have you closed your register yet?"

She shook her head and put Killer down on the floor. She took the book he'd handed her and smiled. "I love this series. I'm afraid I'm a few books behind."

"Urban fantasy is my jam. I found his work in law school, and it was what I rewarded myself with when I'd finish a semester. Thank goodness he had a lot of books in the series to motivate me." He handed her a credit card, and after she'd processed the sale, he took the book and receipt and tucked it under his arm. "Thanks for stocking those books for me."

"Thanks for promoting the bookstore." Rarity followed him to the door and then locked it after him. She turned the sign from *Open* to *Closed* and started turning off lights. She found Killer back in his bed and picked him up. Tucking her tote under her arm, she left the bookstore, making sure to lock it and turn on the alarm. Killer barked as they started walking home.

"Don't look at me that way, he's just a fellow business owner." She held her tote closer and thought about Archer with the gorgeous eyes. She looked down at Killer as they waited for the light to change so they could walk across the street. "I am not ready for a relationship. Besides, I have you. That's all I need for right now."

She just wished she believed what she said.

Holly caught up with her as she passed by Madame Zelda's. "Hey, I was hoping to catch you before you closed up. I'm on my way to work, but I wanted to tell you I know who our local fortune teller was seeing a few nights ago. Kelly O'Reilly. I guess they've been going out for a couple of months, or at least they've been very chummy at the Garnet, according to my friend."

"Interesting." Rarity looked up at the twinkling lights around Madame Zelda's window. "There were numbers for two Kellys in Martha's phonebook. Of course, that doesn't mean either one was the person she was seeing. I didn't find anything that listed off who she was going on her date nights with."

"Well, we have a kind-of match. I guess we could call both the numbers and see what their answering machines say. It might tell us if they had this Kelly in common." Holly sighed as she started walking with Rarity. "And again, even if it is, it could be a coincidence. Or he could be a Realtor or a plumber."

"Yeah, Sam and I were talking about that problem. So we have information, but no context." Rarity paused at her street. "I guess we just keep asking questions and seeing if we can find a way to answer them."

Holly nodded. "You know this investigation stuff looks so much easier on television. They find the killer with the clue that the murder victim left in the sand next to their body. We didn't even get to see the body."

"I'm kind of thankful for that." Rarity waved as they parted ways. "Have a good night at work."

"Will do. I'll need another book to read by tomorrow, though, so put some of your favorites aside for me. I'd love to know what you love reading." Holly jogged across the street to the police station/city hall building.

Rarity thought about Holly's statement. Maybe they needed to know Martha better. Like, find out what she liked to read. Rarity didn't remember whether or not Martha had been in the bookstore before the night of the book club, but if she had, her name and prior purchases would be in the computer. She'd make a note as soon as she got home to check on that tomorrow. And she needed to make a call.

She dialed as she walked, but instead of reaching Sam, she got her recording. "Hey, Sam, you're probably on your way over but I wanted to tell you that Archer came by the store today. He asked me to go on a hiking tour with him on Saturday morning. And you're coming too. Anyway, see you soon!" When she hung up, she tucked her phone into her pocket and focused on Killer the rest of the way home. Talking about the neighborhood and things she wanted to do to the house when she finally got settled. He was a good listener.

Rarity opened the lock on the front door and got their dinners going. Killer's was easy—she just opened a can of wet food, refilled his water dish, and made sure he had dry kibble. The vet would probably tell her that she needed to keep the dry out only at feeding time, but for now, Killer had full-time access to food. Which Rarity thought was the best for all concerned.

Then she put a frozen entrée into the oven and set out the makings for a salad. Happy with her choices, she changed into her swimsuit and went to swim the knots out of her shoulders. She'd spent more on the house for the pool—she was going to get her use out of it.

She saw Sam come out of the house with Killer at her feet. Sam had a bottle of wine and two glasses in her hand. Rarity wasn't surprised to see her. She'd given the extra key to Sam just in case. She paused at the edge of the pool. "I have five more laps unless you need to talk now. Or you can grab a suit from my dresser and join me."

"I'm fine. I ran this morning when it was cool. There's a reason I live in the desert rather than by the ocean. I like my exercise dry, not wet. I'll just pour the wine."

"If you want something to eat, throw an extra frozen dinner into the oven and reset the timer." Rarity went back to swimming without waiting for an answer. Sam was over at her place a lot. Having a friend nearby was so different from when she'd lived in St. Louis. There, she had work friends, but after happy hour, she'd gone home to make dinner for Kevin while they'd gone out to dinner as a group. After a while, they'd stopped asking her to go out with them entirely. She liked having Sam live so close. It reminded her of their college days when they'd shared an apartment. She finished her laps, then climbed out of the pool, drying herself off with a towel as she walked over to the table. She wrapped the towel around herself and sat down.

"Good swim?" Sam filled Rarity's wineglass.

Rarity used a second towel to work on her hair as they were sitting. With the heat, she'd be bone-dry in no time, but she didn't like how her hair dripped down her back if she didn't towel-dry it. "I love that pool."

Sam laughed and sipped her wine. "I grabbed some type of dinner and put it in the oven. So my dinner will be done about ten minutes after yours. Thanks for that."

"You showed up and looked hungry. What could I do?" Rarity sipped her wine. "Did you get my voice mail?"

"About hiking on Saturday? Yes. I'm impressed that you took the initiative and set this up." Sam held up her phone. "I've got it in my calendar."

"I didn't. Archer came by and talked me into going. I'm ordering some books for his customers, and he wanted to walk me through the ones he could recommend."

"You have two guys after you, and I can't even get one to come to breakfast." Sam sipped her wine. "It's like college all over again."

"No, you were the social butterfly in college. I dated three, maybe four guys the whole time."

"True, but everyone wanted to date you. You just didn't see it. You thought they were all just so friendly," Sam groused.

"They were friendly." Rarity smiled, remembering the fun they used to have when they'd go out with a gang of friends. "Anyway, you went to breakfast with one of those two guys you're claiming are hung up on me this morning."

"Only because you kicked him out of the office." Sam nodded. "Yeah, he told us. Did you find anything else out?"

"Holly stopped me on her way to work." Rarity explained what Holly had said and that it didn't rule out anyone from Martha's planner. "We need to find out who these other guys are."

"Let me see the list." Sam stood waiting for directions on what Rarity had done with it.

She pointed inside the house. "On the island."

Sam came out and smoothed the page down on the table. She pointed to one of the numbers in the first phone number. "Okay, what is that number? I can't read your handwriting."

"It's a seven. What are you doing?"

Sam held up a finger and dialed a number. Then she wrote down on the paper a name and company name.

Rarity turned the page to see it. "Roger, from Sedona Plumbing?"

"Yep, and now we're down to four. Don't worry, I'll do the wrong number excuse if anyone really picks up." She dialed the rest of the numbers, hanging up on two and leaving the Kellys until last. On the last call, Sam put the recording on speaker so Rarity could hear it.

The man who answered spoke with a slight Irish brogue. "This is Kelly O'Reilly. Leave a message or don't, I don't care either way."

Sam hung up the phone. "Bingo."

Chapter 10

Sam and Rarity had decided that they'd go together to tell Drew what the group had pieced together. They met outside the bookstore. Rarity called into the store, where she'd left Killer with one of his hidden treat toys. "Killer, I'll be back in a few minutes. Be a good boy."

"I'm not sure he understands those words." Sam chuckled. A few blocks before the police station, Sam backed out. "Just don't tell him I was involved. I hate to have him discount me as a crazy before our first date."

"Do you have a first date planned?" Rarity asked her retreating friend.

Sam shook her head. "Not yet, but if I go in there and tell him we've been snooping, I'm sure there won't be a first, let alone a second or third."

"Sam, you're such a chicken." Rarity crossed the street and went inside the police station. The same woman, Sue, was sitting behind the desk. Her face lit up when she saw Rarity. "Is Drew available?"

"Yes, he is." She stood and knocked over a cup filled with pens. "Oops, sorry about that. Go on over to the door, I'll buzz you in. I'm assuming you know your way to his office?"

"Since I was just here yesterday, I think I can handle finding it." Rarity waved a hand and disappeared into the door that had just beeped open. She wondered how far her friendship with Drew could cover up her attempts to find Martha's killer. Maybe there was a good reason she was pushing this idea. Like her new dog was infiltrating her brain with his ideas. Killer wanted her to find Martha's killer as a last act of respect for his prior owner. Who knew exactly what any dog knew, or if they could think at such an advanced level? Of course, Rarity thought dogs were smarter than most people on the planet.

She found herself outside Drew's door, watching him read a file.

"Come in or go away. Your choice." He looked up and caught her gaze. His eyes were a dark brown color. And the combination with a good tan and comfortable and gently used clothing made her think that he was the good guy she thought he was—and that he might actually believe her.

Longshot number four thousand, four hundred, and thirty-five. She took a deep breath, then went in and sat down. She pulled out a piece of paper that had Kelly O'Reilly's name and phone number on it. She pushed it toward Drew, and he reached across the desk and picked it up.

"What am I looking at?" Drew looked up at her. "Besides the obvious."

"He's a link between Martha and Madame Zelda. They were both seeing him, we think. At worst, he's attached to both women."

Drew stared at her, then took the piece of paper and put it in the file. "I can't just go in guns blazing based on the fact that these two women might have been seeing the same man. This may be Arizona, but it's not the Old West, where the cowboy rides in on a white horse and saves the day."

"All I'm asking is that you talk to Madame Zelda about where she was when Martha died. Rumor is, they had a history, and both their husbands left at the same time." Rarity stood and walked toward the office door. "I can see myself out. Since you're busy."

"Look, I don't know who's feeding you information from the case, but you need to be careful. Murder investigation is a dangerous hobby for a bookseller." He watched her walk toward the door.

Rarity could see him in the reflection of the window by the door. He didn't look angry, he looked amused.

"Hey, tell your friend to come by next week and we'll do coffee without the folks. If she's interested in something other than just matchmaking. I need to know potential dating partners for a while before we move to the dinner-and-a-movie part of the ritual. What if I can't stand her laugh and we're on our way to Flagstaff for a meal? I could be stuck in a truck with a laughing hyena for hours."

She turned and laughed in spite of herself. "Sam's laugh is fine, but I'll pass on your message. I feel like we're in high school again."

"I'm going to go out on a limb, but since you brought it up, are you available for coffee?" His eyes twinkled. "I get the friend thing, so if I'm overstepping, I apologize. I don't want to get involved with one friend when the other is more my type."

"Actually, I'm in a not dating period." She mentally shook her head. Sam had been right after all. "And I'm a pretty loyal friend."

"I've always had bad timing." He nodded. "Have a good day, and thank you for this, I think."

"I'd say let me know what you find out, but then I'd get the lecture about staying out of your investigation. I'll pass your note to Sam." She smiled and left the office, waving at the receptionist as she walked through the lobby and out onto the street. That hadn't been as bad as she'd thought, except the fact he'd asked her for coffee. She liked Drew as a friend, but he didn't push the bells for her. Now, Archer, if he'd asked, then maybe. But she might just be imagining any interest on his part. He might just be drumming up business for his hiking company. She decided her best option was to forget about all men and hurry to the bookstore to open. She needed to be there in case she had customers today. A girl could only hope.

Later that day, the front door blew open, and Madame Zelda stormed inside. "I can't believe you called the cops on me."

"I don't know what you're talking about," Rarity lied as she glanced around the bookstore. Thankfully the last shopper must have just left. "Why would I call the cops?"

"You were at the police station this morning. I saw you when I was running. And then I get a visit from Anderson? Why on earth would you think I killed Martha?" Madame Zelda pounded the counter with a finger. "I was the one who told her to come to your stupid book club. Maybe one of you guys killed her."

"And any of us in the book club would have motive, how?" Rarity shot back.

"Did you even talk to her? Martha was the meanest woman I've ever met. She thought everyone was out to get her and wanted her money. Of course, she didn't have much, but she thought she was loaded. I agreed to read her weekly to try to bring some positivity into her life. And then she actually started dating and bought that dog of yours. I might not have been a good friend all our lives, but I was her only friend." Madame Zelda paused and looked around, then sat down on the bench by the counter. "Look, I'm sorry I came busting in here. I just assumed you'd talked to Anderson."

"You're right, I did." Rarity let that sink in for a minute. "So, if you didn't kill her, who did?"

Madame Zelda stared at her for a full minute. Then she shook her head. "I have no idea. Anderson asked where I'd been Thursday night after eight, which must have been when she died. I had an alibi. And no, I wasn't with Kelly O'Reilly. I had a date with a different man. Anyway, all I can think about was that she was so happy she had kicked cancer's butt a second time."

"Wait, what do you mean, a 'second time'?" Rarity thought about Martha's reaction at the book club.

"She'd gone to a new oncologist, and he found a second lump in her breast. She was doing some new type of experimental treatment. She didn't lose her hair or anything. Just took a pill in the morning and at night. She'd just found out her last set of scans were clear a few weeks ago." Madame Zelda sighed. "It's sad to beat cancer twice and then get killed for no reason at all."

Rarity didn't believe Martha's death was random or motiveless, but she didn't say that to Madame Zelda. "I guess that's why she was so touchy about her cancer history at the meeting. All she wanted to do was talk about the books, not what brought us together."

"Well, yes, and no. Like I said, Martha was like that. Prickly. I used to call her 'Cactus' when we were in school. It didn't matter what you said, she'd take offense." Madame Zelda smiled at the memory. "I'd better get back to the shop. I have readings this afternoon. Thanks for trying to find out who killed Martha. I appreciate it, even if your aim was off-target this time."

"Thanks for coming in to talk. Now I know more." Rarity walked her to the doorway, where Madame Zelda stopped to look back at Killer, who was sitting by the counter, watching them.

"She would have loved you taking care of Killer. She adored that dog." Madame Zelda left the store and hurried over to her own, not looking back.

Rarity closed the door and looked back at Killer. "Well, I guess I need to update our murder book for the next meeting. We get to cross off one suspect. The problem is, we don't have another. Yet."

Sam called that night after dinner, and Rarity told her all the juicy gossip about Madame Zelda. "So then she told me that Killer had a good home with me. Or something like that."

"Wow, I miss all the fun. I can't believe she just ran into your shop and yelled at you for ratting her out." Sam giggled. "I'm so glad I didn't go to the station this morning."

"Brat. Anyway, she has an alibi for the time and date of Martha's death. Which was Thursday after eight, by the way." Rarity rolled back her shoulders. They were aching from unpacking books most of the day. "Maybe I should have opened a store that sold something soft and light. Like a candy store."

"We already have one. And besides, you love books." Sam yawned loud enough that Rarity heard it over the phone.

"You better go. Are we still on for Saturday morning?" Rarity pulled out her calendar. She'd called and made their reservations that morning before she'd chickened out, like Sam had earlier. Except Archer hadn't been the one to take her reservation. It had been a woman who'd answered the phone. Rarity tried not to read anything into that. The woman might just work for him, but it had put a bad taste in her mouth anyway. Especially after her mental gymnastics when Drew had asked her out.

"I'll be there with bells on," Sam responded.

It was after she ended the call that Rarity realized she hadn't told Sam to call Drew about coffee. She'd call back now, but Sam was obviously tired. If Rarity told her now, Sam wouldn't get to sleep. She'd stop by Sam's crystal store tomorrow.

* * * *

Friday morning, Rarity decided to take a swim before going in to the store. Killer sat in the water on the top stair, watching her swim. When she finished her laps, she sat next to him and held him out into the water away from her. He dog-paddled to the step again. She repeated it a few times until she was certain that if he fell in, he could get back out. She didn't let him outside by the pool unless she was with him. But you never knew.

She got dressed, and they headed to the bookstore. There were never any neighbors out when she walked to or from work. She wouldn't even know the houses around her were inhabited, except the music and lights that went off after dark. She hadn't known her neighbors in St. Louis either. But at least she'd seen them out and about.

She walked by the bookstore and went into Sam's crystal shop. The bell rang over the door, and she heard Sam's voice coming out of the back.

"Sorry, we're not quite open. Come back in an hour."

Rarity called out, "Sam, it's me, Rarity."

Sam popped her head out from behind a curtain that covered a doorway. "Sorry, I thought you were a customer. Come on back, if you don't mind the dust."

"Are you cutting rocks?" Rarity hadn't been in Sam's studio before.

"Polishing." She pointed to the table. "I've got to get necklaces made out of all that by the first of the week. We're supposed to have a convention coming into the hotel on Wednesday, and I want to have plenty of stock available."

"What kind of convention?" Rarity picked up a black stone and felt its cool, smooth surface.

"Medical. Either equipment or doctors, but the last time one of these came to town, I sold out of everything. Bored doctor wives have the money to buy nice souvenirs." She pointed to the stone in Rarity's hand. "I'm not surprised you were drawn to that one. It's Shungite, known for its healing properties as well as for cleaning and aligning your molecules. You always pick just the right stone for what you need."

"I just picked it up, you don't have to give it to me." Rarity tried to return it to the table, but Sam wrapped Rarity's fingers around the stone.

"It's yours. It called to you for a reason. Why else would you be here in my shop this morning?"

"Honestly, I came to tell you that Drew said if you wanted to get coffee without the parents, he'd be willing. So now I'm out of it, and you two can make your own love connection." Rarity put the stone in her jeans pocket. It was pretty and somehow, keeping it felt right.

"He did? I really thought he was more interested in you." Sam let the statement hang in the air.

Finally, Rarity caved. "Fine, he asked if I was dating anyone, but I told him no, I was taking a break."

"So, I'm his second choice?" Sam picked up a stone and started to clean it with one of her cloths. "If I wasn't so desperate just to have someone to hang out with, I might be offended."

"Drew's a good guy. And he was already planning on calling you for coffee. Don't go there if you're not serious." Rarity nodded to the clock. "I'd better go and open the shop. I'll see you tomorrow morning?"

"I hear you. I won't break the guy's heart. Anyway, I'll have the coffee ready and waiting." Sam walked with her toward the door. "Look, it must be all this talk about dating, but I've been thinking about this Kelly guy we found in Martha's planner. If he was seeing both Madame Zelda and Martha, maybe he's the killer? Maybe he didn't plan for either of them to find out. And he might not have known they knew each other. It could be that Martha found out, and they got into a fight about his being with both women?"

"Not my case to solve. I did my citizenly duty and pointed Drew to Madame Zelda. It will only take one or two more dead ends for him to think I'm a kook." She paused at the door. "I don't think this will stop our group from investigating more, though, do you?"

"Great idea. I'll call Holly and see if she's around. She's good at this puzzle-solving thing. And it's nice having another friend in the area." Sam looked back at her workshop and sighed. "I'm not sure why I'm wasting my time thinking about Martha's death when I need to be focused on creating more stock. Too many things roaming around in my head."

"My counselor said that balance is all about being fully present in whatever you do. So when you're at work, you focus on work, and when you're home, you focus there." Rarity glanced outside, where the sun was already heating the air. "I'm not sure it works that way."

"It doesn't for me. I'm always worried about something that I can't do anything about. That's why I make lists. It helps me remember what I need to get done." Sam rubbed Killer's head. "I'll see you tomorrow morning. And if I hear anything else about our new suspect, I'll let you know."

"Thanks." Rarity hurried to the sidewalk and then to her bookstore, opening the door, but then setting Killer down in the shade outside. She had a patch of rocks where normally she'd have a small yard. He ran over and watered his favorite rock. Every morning and whenever she let him out, it was the same place, same rock. When he was done, Killer hurried inside and ran to his water bowl to refill. "You're just a pile of trouble, little man, aren't you?"

Killer ignored her and went to his bed, where he found the bone he'd been chewing on yesterday. Another day had begun.

Rarity kind of felt sorry for Kelly O'Reilly if he didn't kill Martha. If he did, she was certain that the powerhouse team of Sam and Holly was going to find out how, where, and why, and have him locked up before he could say *it wasn't me.*

Chapter 11

Rarity sat drinking coffee and talking to Sam the next morning. They were early for the hike, but there were a lot more people milling about today than the last time they'd taken a tour. "Is weekend traffic always this much better than during the week?"

Sam yawned and nodded. "Yes, but it depends. Next week is that conference at the convention center, so a lot of these people are probably here early for the conference."

"That makes sense. Did you talk to Holly?"

"She had to work, so we met up about ten at the Garnet. I stayed up way too late to be hiking this morning." Sam grinned and sipped her coffee. "But Holly's going to see what she can find with an internet search on our Casanova and see if there's any fire to the smoke."

"I just don't see any other motive for Martha's death."

A woman sat down next to her, fanning herself. "I swear if we don't get this thing going, I'm going back to the hotel and ordering room service for the next week. I can watch television without anyone trying to steal the remote from me."

"Sounds like a plan, but you'd miss all the beautiful sights the town offers." Rarity tried to add encouragement. Maybe the woman was a reader, and she could mention her store. "I'm not often out either, and this is my second hike with the company. I loved the first one."

"Honey, you're a lot skinnier and younger than I am." The woman smiled as she fanned herself. She held out a match to the fan she held in her hand. "Here, take a fan. One of the doctors from the convention was handing them out like candy last night at the reception. You'd think he'd save his marketing dollars for those who could send people his way, not a bunch of doctors."

Rarity took it and snapped it open. The sound of it made her smile—it felt like a real Japanese fan. "Thank you. This is really high quality."

"Yeah, the guy said he had thousands made. He would have been better off by getting a real medical degree than just getting a PA degree. Now he's trying to convince medical doctors that he can cure cancer? I may not have a medical degree, but I can smell a rat a mile away." The woman saw Ender pull his bus up to the curb and stood up. "Being a doctors wife means you get the 411 on all the new advancements as well as the fake cures."

Rarity had to smile, the woman was funny. "You sound like you didn't like this guy."

"I didn't. Not one bit. Of course my husband thinks I'm overreacting, but seriously, he's trouble. I thought snake oil salesmen died out with the Great Depression, but instead, they're alive and well and scamming our elderly population in Arizona." She waved. "I'll see you on the trail."

"Well, aren't you just making friends." Sam joined her and leaned forward to read the fan. "Donald Conrad, 'medical specialist in cutting-edge cancer recovery treatments.' Well, at least he's not claiming to be a doctor. I hear that's kind of a no-no."

Rarity held the fan down. "Yeah, but it does feel kind of scammy, doesn't it? I've heard there are all kinds of people out there trying to say they know the cure for cancer. No chemo, no surgery, no pills, just use this lotion or do yoga. And of course, think positive."

"Come on, folks, let's get moving. The bus will leave in five minutes, so if you're not on it, there's no refunds," Archer called from the steps of the bus. He met Rarity's gaze and smiled. Then he disappeared back inside the bus.

"Well, I guess that's our cue." Sam took the fan and threw it in the trash. "You don't need that. You've paid your dues."

Rarity followed Sam to the bus, but she turned once to stare at the trash can where Sam had thrown the fan. What was bothering her about the guy? The fact that he was playing on other people's fears? Or was it more?

"Rarity? Are you okay?" Sam asked from the bus stairs.

She hadn't noticed that she'd stopped walking while she tried to ferret out the connection. She shook her head and hurried to catch up. "I'm fine. Just woolgathering I guess."

Just like the last hike, the next few hours were filled with beauty and a good workout. Sam and Rarity were sipping water at the halfway point when Archer joined them. "Are you enjoying the hike?"

"It's so beautiful here." Rarity glanced around the small area where they'd stopped. "I can't believe any place on earth looks like this."

"It started as a cattle trail, then was upgraded to a wagon trail. Lots of history in this one spot." He squatted down and picked up dust from the trail. "Who knows whose boots have walked here before?"

"You like history?" Rarity asked.

"I love it. I was a history minor in college, but I knew I couldn't make any money as a high school teacher. And I didn't want to stay in school long enough to get my master's. But I still write articles now and then. It's fun." He stood and kicked at a rock in the trail. "Are you enjoying yourself?"

"Yes, we are." She stepped toward Sam, who was watching the two of them chatter. "This is my friend I told you about. Sam, this is Archer Ender."

"You run the gem shop." He held out a hand to shake. "I've bought some things to give as gifts there. Your work is very popular in my family."

"That's nice to hear, and thank you for your support." She shook his hand. "I love living here in Sedona. It always feels just a little different, even if you've been on the same trail before."

"I'm not sure I could live anywhere else." He looked at his watch and then to his assistant. "Time to get this group heading back. I bet you two need to open your stores soon."

"I'm hoping for a strong weekend, so yes, I guess I'd better get moving." She glanced around the area one more time. "But it is breathtaking. I hate to leave."

"Then you'll just have to come back again." He pulled a piece of paper from his pocket. "Did those books come in yet?"

"I've got them stocked and a sign on the counter saying, *Ask me about trail books*." She took the paper. "What's this?"

He nodded. "I'm giving one to everyone as they leave the bus. It's a map to your store and a list of the hiking books you have for sale. I wanted to wait until I saw you to make sure the books came in. Hopefully this will help steer some business your way."

Sam glanced over at the paper after he left. "That's a nice promotion. I wish I had a trail rock available."

"Well, if they come to the bookstore, I bet they'll stop by your shop on the way in or out." She tucked the paper into her pocket.

"It's nice to have other businesses help drive traffic." Sam started down the trail following the crowd.

"Yes, it was sweet of him." Rarity followed her down the path.

"Yes, it was. Very sweet." Sam didn't look at her, but Rarity could tell her friend was grinning.

* * * *

On Sunday the shop was closed, so Rarity hung around the house. She swam in the morning, then puttered with a cookie recipe she'd been meaning to try. She needed to settle in and read, but she kept thinking about the hike. Archer had been right—it had been something she needed to see. Maybe she should send him a thank-you note. Or call him.

Except she only had the trail hiking company's number. It might look wrong if Archer's girlfriend was the one acting as a receptionist. Except if he had a girlfriend, wouldn't he have told her? Not that it would be something to come up in conversation. Especially since they'd just talked about hiking, hiking books, and Sedona.

Killer watched her from his perch on the back of the couch. She pointed her finger at him. "If you're not careful, someone will think you're a cat."

He barked but got down and curled up on the cushion for his nap.

Rarity decided she was going to join him and took a glass of tea over to where a book lay that needed reading. She picked it up and fell into the story.

On Monday the shop didn't open until late, so she spent the morning in Flagstaff grocery shopping, then stopped at the pet store to bring Killer home a treat. After dropping over a hundred dollars there, she decided it was time to head back to Sedona. Pets were expensive. Especially when you started buying toys. She'd wanted to get him an outfit, but in Sedona's heat, the only place he'd wear it was inside. Maybe she'd buy him some outfits for the holidays and he could be the store's mascot?

She was singing along with the radio when her phone rang. Seeing it was Sam, she picked up using the Bluetooth in her car. "Are you done with your stock?"

"What? No. I'm still working on the last fifty pieces. Anyway, Holly found out something. Apparently, Mr. O'Reilly works for a real estate company."

Rarity waited for the punch line, but when one didn't come, asked, "So?"

"He was probably trying to buy Martha and Madame Zelda's place. Real estate people are always coming into the shop and trying to get me to sell for a lowball offer."

"Just because he's a Realtor doesn't mean he was trying to buy either woman's property. Or maybe he did meet them that way, but then he could have fallen in love. Love happens, you know." Rarity passed a large cactus by the side of the road. No matter how many times she saw the tall cactus, she thought of the old Westerns her mom used to like to watch.

"Oh, we're thinking about love, are we?" Sam teased.

"Shut up. I'm not thinking about love. I'm just saying that maybe Martha and this Kelly guy were in love." She looked in the rearview mirror and saw she was grinning. Crap, Sam was right. She was thinking about Archer.

"Anyway, I just wanted to warn you that we're going to use some of the book club time tomorrow night to set up a murder board for what we know. Shirley's bringing a whiteboard we can keep in the back and use for our meetings."

"You all are nuts." Rarity turned off the highway and into town. "I'll see you tomorrow night. I just turned into town. I'm sure Killer's waiting."

"See you then. I need to finish my work so I can come and play tomorrow. This is fun." Sam disconnected the call.

Rarity drove by the police station. "I bet Drew would hate to hear you say that."

On a whim, she turned the car into a parking lot on the right and shut off the engine. She had her perishable groceries in a cooler, so she had a little time before her grocery run would go to waste. O'Reilly's Homes was set in a stucco building that looked like it had been in Sedona forever. The clay-tile roof set off the tan color of the building, and someone had decorated the outside with brightly colored weathervanes and wind chimes. She heard the tinkle of the pipes as she walked up to the door. When she turned the knob, it opened. Closing her eyes, she thought of what she was going to say before pushing the door open. Maybe something like, "Hi, did you know Martha Redding? Were the two of you dating? And did you kill her?" Maybe she'd leave off that last question. She could have Drew ask it. Oh heck, she'd just wing it.

She pushed open the door and stepped into an air-conditioned lobby. A sign at the window announced that no one was on-site, but she was welcome to peruse the listings available from the flyers or online. The lights to the office behind a closed window were off, and there was only one interior door. It was locked. She realized that this was the twenty-four-seven section of their marketing strategy. The front door was always open, but the offices were actually closed for the day. She thought about leaving a note but couldn't come up with the right wording. Especially since she'd decided not to ask the *are you a killer* question.

Just in case they had cameras and checked the feed, she took a couple of flyers, then left and went back to her car. She tucked the flyers into one of the grocery bags and went home to put away the food before she didn't have any ice cream left.

* * * *

Tuesday night, everyone was at the bookstore a full thirty minutes before the meeting and they'd brought something to eat. Shirley had her whiteboard and cupcakes. Holly and Malia had brought a spicy cheese dip with chips. And Sam had made mini sandwiches.

Only Kim had come empty-handed. She saw the potluck the others had set up and frowned. "I didn't realize we were bringing food tonight. I would have stopped at the store for something. I was in town for a doctor appointment today."

"No worries, Kim. We know you have a lot on your plate. You can bring cookies next week if you'd like or not. You just need to focus on getting well." Shirley put an arm around the woman and gave her a little squeeze.

Kim's eyes narrowed, and for a second, Rarity thought she was going to bark out something about "don't touch me" or "leave me alone," but then her face softened. "You all are too good to me."

Everyone called out their support for the woman, but Rarity held back. Something was off with Kim. Maybe she was feeling left out of the group because no one had called her to bring something, but like Shirley said, everyone knew what a long, hard road she had ahead of her.

"Kim, when are they starting your treatments?" Rarity asked.

Kim turned around to meet her gaze. "What?"

"You said you were just at the doctor's. When do your treatments start? I bet we'd all like to support you. Maybe give you rides to chemo or make dinners for you and your husband that week?" Rarity watched as Kim processed the question.

"Actually, they are still discussing the right path. I'm sure I'll find out at my next appointment." Kim hurried over to the treat table. "But for right now, I'm eating one of these cupcakes before they tell me I can't eat sugar or something stupid."

"More likely you won't like the taste of it," Malia offered. "When I went through chemo, I couldn't eat meat at all. I had to take iron pills because I got so anemic."

"That's because you don't like spinach." Holly curled her legs up underneath her on the couch. "I added spinach to my smoothies. It hides the flavor."

"Anyway, what did everyone think of the book?" Kim returned to the group and sat down, holding her book up to try to change the subject.

"Hold your horses. Rarity hasn't joined us yet." Malia pointed out.

"I'll be right there." Rarity left the counter and went to the front door. For someone who wanted to be part of the survivors' group, Kim really didn't like talking about cancer or treatments at all. Or sharing her story, Rarity thought as she set up the sign. She didn't know why she bothered—she rarely had a customer after five. She might just change her hours except for book club nights. That way she and Killer could get home earlier and maybe she could get in a swim every night. "Sorry about taking so long. So how was everyone's week?" She held up a hand. "Hold off on answering that. I need to ask you all a question first. Who's the best cancer doc in town? I need to go for a checkup, and I haven't even tried to set up an appointment."

Shirley pulled out her notebook and ripped off a sheet of paper. "I'll give you the name and number of my oncologist. He has a few others with him, and they have an office in Flagstaff."

"Perfect." Rarity leaned back. "So how has everyone's week gone?"

Kim held up a hand. "I hear Dr. Conrad's really good."

"Add him to the list." Rarity pointed to Shirley. "I like having options."

"Sometimes too many choices gives you conflicting information. You really should try Dr. Conrad." Kim ignored the sheet of paper Shirley was pushing toward her.

"Everyone has their own opinion on things. That's fine. Besides, I'm just looking for someone to check in with once a year. Not someone to walk me through treatment." Rarity wondered why Kin was pushing so hard. Especially since Doctor Conrad was the man with the fan. She turned toward Malia. "Tell us, what's been going on with you?"

Everyone had a bit of info to share about their lives as they went around the room. When it was Kim's turn, she shook her head. "I've already told you all what's going on. I'm in a holding pattern."

"That's so frustrating," Holly added. "When you're first looking for a doctor, it takes forever to get in with them, but now they're dragging their feet? What are they thinking?"

"Measure twice, cut once," Shirley said.

Everyone turned to look at her.

"What, haven't you heard that saying?" Shirley pulled her afghan out of her tote and started crocheting.

"I've heard it, I'm just not sure what it means in this situation." Malia watched Shirley's fingers fly as she manipulated the yarn and needle.

"It means that they're being cautious with our friend Kim's treatment, and I, for one, think it's a fantastic idea. You don't want to turn your life over to someone who doesn't think about their actions and reactions."

Shirley smiled in Kim's direction. "We want to be part of the treatment or the solution, right?"

"Let's discuss the book so we can talk about Martha. I want to use that white board and take notes on things we've found out about the murder." Holly held up the book. "I'll start. I really liked the main character, but her friend, she seemed fake."

The "book" part of the book club took less than fifteen minutes, including picking a new book to read. Then the group got down to the real reason they were all there. To talk about murder.

Chapter 12

Rarity hadn't gotten out of the bookstore until after ten. So, when her alarm went off the next morning, she reached over and tapped it with one hand. After snoozing it for several rounds, she finally turned it off and rolled over to see Killer staring at her. "I suppose you need to go outside?"

He barked and turned three circles on the bed, his way of saying yes.

"Okay, fine, but you need to do your thing and come right back in. I don't have time for this." She peered at the clock. It was almost eight. She climbed out of bed and slipped a light robe over her old T-shirt and panties. Her favorite set of pj's ever. "I need coffee."

She let Killer out, thinking that one of these days she was going to have to install a dog door. Especially since Killer was officially part of the family now. Or he would be when she took him to the vet and had official records saying Killer belonged to her. She felt like she'd won the adoptive dog mom lottery. But as soon as she thought that, she felt bad about Martha. It was a vicious cycle.

She planned out her next book order as the coffee brewed, writing the plan in her notebook. Her doorbell rang. She walked over to the front door and looked out the side window. Drew Anderson stood there, watching her watch him. She pulled the door open. "What did I do wrong now?"

He held up a bag and the aroma of fresh donuts filled Rarity's foyer. "I just wanted to talk. And see Killer. I brought a peace offering."

"I appreciate that. Do you want coffee? I can't chat for long, I've got to get the store opened."

"I forgot you were opening so soon." Drew glanced at his watch. "I'm not disturbing you, am I?"

"No, all I need to do is get dressed and pack up Killer's go bag. Then I'll be ready." She opened the sliding-glass door, and Killer came inside. "The coffee's not ready yet. Give me five minutes, and I'll be right back out. I'll feel more comfortable if I'm dressed when Sedona's finest is chatting with me over nothing."

"I didn't say it was nothing." He let his mouth curve into a smile and waved her away. "Go on, get dressed. I'll get my coffee when it's done brewing. Are the cups over the coffee pot?"

"Of course, where else would they be?" She hurried into her room to change. When she came back out, no one was in the kitchen or the living room. She followed sounds out to the deck, where two cups of coffee sat on the table with a plate of donuts between them and a pile of napkins nearby. Drew was playing tug-of-war with Killer. "Looks like he's winning."

Drew let go of the rope, and Killer took his hard-won gains over to his dog bed on the deck, prancing all the way. "I let him win."

"I'd stick with that story if I were you." She sat and sipped her coffee.

"I hoped black was fine? I didn't see any sugar out or creamer in the fridge." Drew leaned back in his chair, picking up his own coffee cup.

"Oh, you've been in my fridge? Did you find anything interesting?"

He grunted. "You have food in there. I'm surprised. Before my folks moved in, my fridge was pretty empty except for pizza boxes and cans of soda. I'm not much of a cook. It was what I found in your trash can when I threw away the donut bag that I thought was interesting."

She tried to remember what could be in her trash but failed. "Okay, it's too early for my speed round of trivia. What was in my trash?"

Drew pulled from his shirt pocket one of the flyers for a three-bedroom loft on Main Street. "Are you thinking of selling this place? If you are, I want to know. I'll have to take on a second job, but if it gets me away from my parents, I'll do it."

"You'd move out of your own house and buy a second place just to avoid telling them they'd overstayed their welcome?" She took one of the donuts. "Someone needs to grow up."

"Actually, I'm grown-up. I just don't like to hurt my parents. And that's why I'm here. I need you to talk to my dad." He grabbed a donut and a napkin. "Then filter what he says. Just answer my questions without giving me any more details than what I ask for."

"Wait, you want me to talk to your dad? About what?" Rarity tore the donut in half. She ate half and set the second part down. Then she sipped more coffee to cut the sweet flavor in her mouth. She was going to have a sugar headache as soon as she finished the other half of the donut. Of course, she could just not eat the other half, but what was the fun in that? She watched as Drew dropped his gaze, and she saw his cheeks blaze red. Oh yeah, this was priceless.

"I was going through Martha's planner, and I saw that Dad's name and phone number are in it. And they have a star by them." He ran a hand through his hair. "I can't just ask him over coffee with my mom sitting right there. What if...he and Martha were...well, were..."

Rarity watched him struggle with even the idea that his father might have had an affair. "Look, your dad didn't seem that type to me when I was talking to him on the hike. He looked at your mom like she was the only female on the planet. Maybe he was helping Martha with something? Where would she have met him anyway?"

"Church. They're in the same adult Bible study. Mom sleeps in on Sunday mornings and meets him at the eleven o'clock service. So that might explain the name and number in her journal, but geez, what if something more was happening?" He grabbed another donut and tore a bite off it. "If he and Martha were an item, well, I couldn't look him in the eye ever again. And I'd have to tell my mom, which would kill her. They were high school sweethearts."

"So, you want me to find out exactly how your dad knows Martha and whether or not he killed her, but not find out whether they were having an affair." Rarity tried to summarize what he'd said.

"Yes. Or at least if you find out, don't tell me. I know he didn't kill her, so I'll need an alibi for a certain time. So, if you could ask him that, too, that would be great." He gave her a slip of paper that had times written down with a date. "I want to know everything except whether or not his relationship with Martha was more than just friends."

"So, why me?" Rarity sipped her coffee and watched for his response.

He turned back to her and shrugged. "I can't ask any of the patrol guys to do it. They'd never let me live it down. I'd get teased all the time. Besides, you and I are friends."

She considered his words. She felt like they could be friends. And she couldn't see any trap in the idea. "Okay, but if I need a favor, I expect you to do it without any questions asked."

"I'm already going to coffee with your friend. What else do you want of me?" Drew smiled and leaned back in his chair again. Now that he'd brought up the idea of her questioning his father about a possible connection with Martha, he had relaxed again.

"That's not a favor for me. That's for your mom," Rarity pointed out. "And I don't know yet. I'll let you know when I do."

He nodded solemnly. "Fair enough. Anyway, why were you at O'Reilly's Homes yesterday?"

"Who said I was?" She avoided eye contact and instead watched Killer. Who was watching her? She must be putting off some sort of danger vibes for someone to be so interested in her.

Drew tapped on the paper. "Besides this? I got a call from a neighbor that someone broke in yesterday and left in a blue Jeep, but when I got there, the place was empty. I called Kelly, and he said he thought they had forgotten to lock the front door."

"The front door was open. I didn't break in." The words came out before she could consider what consequences her actions—and her honesty—could have. "It looked like they wanted people to look through their listings when they weren't there."

"It used to be that way, but they'd been having issues with break-ins this last year, so they started locking the front. I guess they didn't redo their signage. And before you go back today to see if you can 'chat' with Kelly, he's coming in to talk to me at one. So stop investigating."

"Who said I was investigating? I might have been looking for a house for a friend. And does that mean you don't want me to talk to your father?" Rarity reminded him.

"Okay, stop investigating after you talk to Dad. Just be careful out there. It's not safe if there's really a killer out and about. Even if it is a small town. People die here just like they do in the city." He stood and held up his coffee cup. "Thanks for this. When you know what's going on, call me and we'll do coffee. I'll tell my folks they've convinced me to try to start dating again."

"Just not with the girl they tried to set you up with? No way. Besides, I don't want them thinking it's a real date. I don't need the drama." She followed him into the house, taking the last donut with her. "Do you want this donut?"

He held out his hand to take it. "Thanks for the help and the coffee."

"Thanks for the donuts." She went out on the porch to watch him drive away. A woman stood on the porch next door. Rarity waved, but the woman ignored her and went back inside. So much for being neighborly. She went back inside and filled her travel mug. Then she put Killer on his leash and grabbed his go bag along with her own tote.

"Time to go to work." She and Killer started their morning trip to the bookstore.

For a Wednesday, the store was busy. People came in and out all day, buying not only the most recent bestsellers, but also many of the recommended hiking books. As she talked with the customers, she realized that most of her business was due to the medical convention that was in town.

"So, are you a doctor?" she asked one woman who bought five books from Rarity's curated healing section and had been chatting about Sedona's mystical powers with a friend for a few minutes while Rarity finished helping the customer before.

"Actually, my husband is. I'm the supportive wife now. My role used to be to bring in the money while he was in school, but now I'm free to do anything I choose. So, I look up alternative healing solutions for his problem cases. It's kind of fun." The woman handed Rarity a credit card. "Your healing section is really well stocked. I had to call several bookstores before I found some of those books, and these were all unavailable. Do you have a card or a website? I'd like to check with you first when I need new reference material. I think you'll save me a ton of time."

"Thanks. That's nice to hear. I've been interested in alternative healing ever since I had cancer about a year ago. When you're going through that, you tend to grab at all sorts of promises. But I found most of the miracle cures were just smoke and mirrors." She rang up the purchases and put the books into a bag. She held up a bookmark. "My phone number is on there. I don't have a website yet."

"And yet you live here." The woman took her credit card from Rarity and tucked it in her purse. "I think you must believe in some magic."

As she closed the bookstore that night, she was surprised to see that Sam's store was already dark. Maybe she'd gone to the hotel to man a table in the lobby. Friendship, that was the magic Rarity believed in and the reason she'd pulled up her life from St. Louis and moved to Sedona. A fresh start in a place where she had at least one friend. She should have told the woman today that. She was always thinking afterward about the things she should have said. Killer pulled at his leash and barked. "Okay, boy, I get it. Time to go home and eat dinner."

Now she just had to figure out how to talk to Drew's dad about Martha.

* * * *

On Thursday morning, Rarity was at the bookstore reshelving more hiking books and thinking about the order she needed to place after a very good two days when Jonathon Anderson walked in the door. The bookstore was quiet for the first time that morning. "Good morning, what brings you in today?" she asked.

"I told you I needed some reading material when we were hiking. It just took me a while to get down here. I swear, Edith keeps a tight hold on my strings. She's always thinking of new activities we need to try. I never thought retirement would be so busy." Jonathon scanned the shelves. "I'm looking for some backlist books from one of my favorite thriller authors. I just found him a few months ago, and I've been trying to get caught up."

"Well, let's see what we can dig up. I probably can order anything I don't have in stock. And you picked a good day to visit. My latest order goes in at five." She walked around the counter and pointed to the left side of the bookstore. "That section is over on the side wall. I'll bring my tablet, and we can look up books as we go."

"You're pretty hands-on for a bookstore owner. Usually in the big-box stores, I only see someone when I go to check out." He followed her to the thriller section. "Here we go, he's got quite a backlist, doesn't he?"

She smiled and nodded. It was fun to see a reader realize their favorite author had been publishing for years before they'd found the latest book. "He's very popular. Do you know which ones you've already read?"

Jonathon pulled out a piece of paper from his pocket. "I have a list right here. Should I start with the first one and go forward or the next most recent?"

"That's up to you, but I like reading them in order, so I learn more about the characters and their motivations." She checked her tablet. "It looks like we have the first three in stock. Or you could just browse and see what pulls at you."

He shook his head. "Nope, I'm going to follow your direction and start with book number one. Drew says you're smart, so I guess I should take his recommendation. He doesn't talk about many people here. Are you two dating? Is that why he wasn't interested in the setup his mom made for him?"

"Actually, no, Drew and I are just friends." Rarity thought about the word *friends*, but she decided it was true, even though they'd just met. They were friends. Comfortable in each other's company, with many of the same interests. "And I hear he's considering dating Sam. She and I are friends, too, so even if I was interested in Drew, Sam was my first friend and there's a loyalty factor there. Anyway, back to the books. It looks like I don't have four and five in the series, but I have six and seven. Do you want me to order the missing two?"

"Please. I'll take the first three and come back for more when I'm through with them." He took the books off the shelf and studied the back covers. Without looking at her, he continued their conversation. "I'm sorry if I was too personal back there. Edith just wants to see Drew happy, and she's convinced being in a relationship is just what he needs."

Rarity laughed as she added the next two books to her order for the week. "From what I know of your son, he's pretty aware of what makes him happy. I think our generation just doesn't get married as early as yours did. We have to be convinced a relationship is forever."

"Is that why you're still single?" He followed her to the counter and set the books down.

She considered how to answer his question. If she hadn't gotten diagnosed with cancer, she would have been married by now. To a guy whom she'd found out wouldn't stick with her in the hard times. "Actually, I was on the path to marrying Mr. Wrong a few years ago. A few things happened that let me know he wasn't the one. So now I'm just taking care of me. I'm open to the idea of marriage—I just don't think it's the right time."

"And after your cancer scare, you want to be sure." Jonathon pulled out his credit card. "I understand. There have been times in my life when I questioned whether Edith and I were 'meant to be.' Whether or not she was my soul mate. But I always come back to the fact that our lives together are what we make of them. Don't hold out for a fantasy when real life is more rewarding."

"Thank you for the purchase and the advice. I'll think about it." She tucked his books in the bag and thought if she was going to ask, this probably was the best time she'd ever get. "You said you questioned the fact that Edith was your soul mate. I understand you and Martha were friends. Was she someone you thought might be a soul mate if you weren't married?"

"Martha?" He started laughing and shook his head. "No, Martha Redding was more of a pain in my backside than a potential soul mate, or even a friend. We were in the same Bible study class, and she found out that I'd worked in construction before. So, every time something broke at her house, I was the first one she called. I replaced all her faucets and rebuilt her deck railing. Whoever buys that house from the estate will at least have most of the updates done."

"Oh, I guess I'd heard wrong." At least Drew wasn't going to have to worry about his dad having a relationship with another woman. Or him killing her. "She just had so few friends, I thought maybe."

"I guess we were both wrong with our assumptions, now, weren't we?" He leaned on the counter. "I can't believe someone murdered her. According to what Drew can tell us, he doesn't even have a suspect. The woman was caustic, which was why she didn't have friends, but no one deserves to be killed over the way they approach others. From what I knew about her, she only loved one thing. The little dog you're now taking care of."

"Killer's a great dog." Rarity glanced over to where Killer was sleeping by the fireplace. "He's totally taken over my heart."

Jonathon smiled over at the dog. "He's a good dog. He's very loyal and not a bad watchdog for his size. Tiny, but mighty, at least in his bark. One day I was working on the deck, and Martha had a visitor. Killer went off and wouldn't stop barking until this other guy left. He didn't like him one bit. Which was odd, since Killer seemed to love men. Or maybe it was just me. I have a way with dogs and other wild animals."

After Jonathon left, Rarity thought about his words. She added him to her notes in her investigation book. Maybe someone from the group could collaborate his 'I'm just a handyman' story. The good news was, she didn't have to tell Drew his dad was a cheater. At least, she believed his story. Though, if Jonathon was a cheater, he probably was also a good liar. Would he lie to someone he barely knew? Killer came over and pawed at her leg, telling her he needed a quick walk out to the back alley.

She put up a *BE RIGHT BACK* sign and locked the front door. The sidewalk outside her store was empty, so it was a good time to let Killer do his business. She grabbed baggies and a leash and headed to the back door.

In the alley, she walked in the shade, where the sun wouldn't heat her up any more than the air already was. It also kept Killer's feet off the burning pavement. He nosed around, barked at a bird who landed in his way, then explored some more. Rarity was lost in thought as she considered Jonathon's words. Especially the ones about how he'd thought Drew liked her. She really needed to make sure Sam understood that she and Drew were just friends. At least on her part.

Killer barked and rubbed his face against her pants. She found the present he was announcing and cleaned it up, dumping the bag into her trash can, then she opened the back door to the shop. She saw something out of the corner of her eye and stopped. Was Sam's back door open?

She walked over to Sam's building and checked. The back door was open a crack. She opened it farther and called inside. "Sam? Sam, are you there?"

No answer.

She reached for her phone in her back pocket but realized she'd left it in the bookstore. She picked Killer up and pushed open the door. Maybe her fear was because they'd just been talking about Martha's murder. Or maybe it was because she hadn't talked to Sam since Tuesday night, but she grew more and more concerned as she walked through the empty shop.

She paused at the front door and checked the sign. Relief flooded through her when she read the message Sam had left. She *was* manning a table at the hotel through Friday. She must have just left the back door open accidentally.

She blew out a breath, and Killer whined. "It's okay, Sam is just working somewhere else. We'll call her and let her know we locked the back door for her."

Rarity made her way back to the curtain separating the shop from Sam's studio. Before she walked through, she heard the slam of the back door. She peeked inside the studio to find that the door she'd left standing open was now shut. Someone else had been inside Sam's studio. She stepped back and, using the store phone, dialed 911.

When the dispatcher answered, she spoke calmly and quietly into the receiver. "This is Rarity Cole. I'm in Sam's crystal shop, and I think someone broke in and just left. I'm afraid to go out through the back door. I don't know what I'll find there."

Chapter 13

Drew stood next to her in the alley. The heat was causing drops of sweat to run down her face. She'd given up the idea of wearing makeup when she'd moved here because of the heat. During her call, the dispatcher had told her to stay where she was, so when Drew and another officer came to the front door, Rarity had let them inside. While she'd waited for the police to show up, she'd tried to call Sam three times using the store phone, but each time it had gone directly to voice mail. She didn't know where her friend was, but now she was worried. She still held a shaking Killer in her arms. He was going crazy worrying about her reactions. "Have you heard from the hotel yet?"

"My guys just got there." Drew pulled her into a hug. "She's going to be there. Don't worry."

"All I can do is worry. I can't believe I didn't try to call her last night when I got home. I was just so tired after a busy day in the shop." Rarity blamed herself for not reaching out. Right now, if Sam was missing, the last time she'd seen her was Tuesday night. She and her kidnapper could be in New York or Mexico or Canada by now.

"Look, did you close the bookstore? I hate to think people are milling around waiting for a clerk to show up." He smiled, and she realized he was joking with her.

"Yes, I locked the front door to the bookstore. I said I'd be right back, but that was a half hour ago." She turned to her back door. "Maybe I should go reopen? If I act like nothing's wrong, maybe that's what will happen."

"There's no reason for you to be out here in the heat. I'll let you know as soon as I find her." His phone buzzed as he started walking her toward her shop door. He glanced at it and smiled. "Sam's at the hotel. She said she was at the shop this morning and must have forgotten to lock the door."

All the tension in Rarity flooded out of her. "Thank goodness."

They paused at the back door, and she let Killer down inside. He hurried into the main part of the shop. "Look, I'll go talk with her and make sure everything's all right. We have someone coming to take prints, since it appears someone was inside when you were. Probably some bored local kid."

"I'm so glad. Sorry to have bothered you and your guys." She paused at the door. "Come by when you get off work tonight. I need to talk to you."

He nodded. "Sounds like a plan."

She went inside, and after locking the back door, she went back into the front and unlocked that door. Then she went back to her ordering. Her heart was still beating faster than usual, but she was trying to calm down and not think about what could have happened. Sam was fine, and whoever had been in her studio was gone now. The police would lock up the back door, and Sam could let them know if anything had been taken. Everything was back in order.

So why did she still feel like someone was watching over her shoulder?

A knock sounded at her door exactly at six. Rarity had just gotten home, as there had been a rush at the bookstore just before she'd closed up. Everyone wanted to talk about the break-in. She didn't have much to add to the rumor mill, but she sold at least one book to each of the twenty people who'd wandered in to chat.

She opened the door, and Drew stood there with a takeout bag from one of the local diners. Rarity thought it was some sort of pasta with red sauce and bread sticks from the smell. "We're going to start people talking if you keep bringing me dinner."

He grinned and walked past her. "Wouldn't be the worst thing they could gossip about. Besides, it was either eat with you now or not at all. I've got to go back to the station. One of the beat cops found a homeless guy with one of your friend's bags over in the park. He had it stuffed with metal that he was probably going to Flagstaff to sell for meltdown."

"Well, at least Sam will get it back. I know we have insurance for these types of things, but it's hard to get past the feeling of being violated. I'm just glad she wasn't there and in his way." She pulled out plates and silverware.

"We could eat on paper plates, so you don't have to do dishes." Drew set the bags in the middle of the table, frowning at the china she'd set on the table.

"You're kidding, right? Anyway, using dishes makes it feel like a real meal. If I eat out of a bag, I feel like I'm hungry sooner. I think there's something to be said for eating at the table. Besides, we have things to discuss, and I don't want you spilling food on my carpet when you hear what I have to say." She opened the fridge. "I have iced tea or cola."

"I'll take the cola." He took the containers out of the bag. "So, it's bad? The stuff with my dad?"

"How do you know that's what I needed to talk to you about?" She set two sodas on the table, then sat down in one of the chairs. It was nice to have someone to talk to after a long day at work. Even though Drew wasn't her type, he was excellent company.

"Okay, I'll back up a little." He sat down and started dishing out ravioli. "I got cheese ravioli with red sauce and a clam fettuccine. I figured we could share both, unless you've got a preference."

"I love both. Thanks." She opened the other container, and the cream sauce almost made her cry. "This smells divine."

"One of my favorite restaurants in town. And you can't get more authentic Italian unless you go to Phoenix." He switched containers with her. "I also got two small green salads and a sleeve of bread sticks. So, what did you want to talk about?"

Rarity dished up some of the fettuccine, then set the container down. There was enough for three or four people in the container. "Your dad. He came in today, and we started talking about Martha."

He waited for her to finish the bite she took right after speaking to say, "And he said?"

She wiped clam sauce off her chin. "This food is amazing. Anyway, he said that, like you hoped, he and Martha knew each other from Bible study. The only 'benefits' side of that friendship was on her side with his ability to help her fix her house."

She told him the entire conversation, but then she paused.

"What?" Drew's sharp observation skills had caught her hesitancy. "What aren't you saying?"

She set down her fork and took a drink. "I don't know. Or at least I can't put my finger on it. He was holding back something. No, I don't think he was having an affair, but he knows more about Martha's disappearance than he's saying. I think you need to talk to him. You're better at this than I am."

He shook his head. "Not when it's my father. Thanks for talking to him. I'll have him stop by the station and have a chat. I know he's not guilty of murder, but you and I both know that not guilty is different than totally innocent. Maybe he knows something that he doesn't think is important."

She watched as he finished his dinner, then went to the sink and rinsed his dish. "Are you leaving?"

"Long night ahead with this homeless guy. I just hope he confesses early to get a bunk at the jail. He knows he won't be charged with much more than petty larceny, since what he took wouldn't get him much money. And if Sam left the door open, like we think, he can't even be charged with breaking and entering." He rubbed Killer's ears. "Who's a good boy?"

Killer didn't get time to answer before the front door burst open and Sam hurried into the front room. She froze when she saw Drew standing there.

He smiled. "Hello, Sam."

"Drew." Sam glanced at Rarity, who still sat at the table, a bread stick in her hand. "Rarity. I'm sorry to interrupt your dinner."

"No problem," Drew said. "I've got to leave anyway. Thanks for the favor, Rarity. I appreciate you talking with him." He gave Killer one last rub on his head, then put his hat on and left through the front door.

"Do you want something to eat?" Rarity stood and got another plate. "Drew brought over way too much food."

Sam watched as Rarity set the clean plate down with silverware. She sighed and slipped into the chair Drew had just vacated. She pointed at Rarity's drink. "Do you have another soda?"

"Of course." She got a soda out, and they sat and ate for a bit in quiet.

Finally, Sam pushed her plate away. "I love Antonio's. Why did Drew bring you dinner?"

"He had asked me earlier to talk to his dad about his relationship with Martha." Rarity offered Sam one of the two remaining bread sticks. She took it. "So, when his dad came to the bookstore today, I asked him Drew's questions. I don't blame Drew for not wanting to find out if his dad was a cheater."

"*Was* he a cheater?"

Something in Sam's tone made Rarity turn and focus on her rather than enjoying the last bread stick. "I don't think so. He's hiding something, but he claims that he and Martha were just Sunday school classmates, and he did some handyman work for her at her house."

Sam set down her fork. "The rumor mill said he's been over there a lot."

"According to Jonathon, she called him a lot." Rarity shook her head. "I had twenty locals in my store today wanting to find out gossip about what happened at your shop. I think the rumor mill is way too active in this town. The good thing is, I sold a ton of books to them."

Sam laughed and picked up her fork again. Then she set it down. "The rumor mill said that Drew was over here for breakfast today."

"He was. I told him that if he didn't stop bringing food every time he came by, people would start to talk. I've never seen anyone in the house to my right before this morning, and they just happened to be out when Drew left? Seriously? People need to mind their own business." Rarity finished her salad and then took her plate to the kitchen. "I've got ice cream if you want dessert too."

"Ice cream sounds good," Sam said. "Maybe with some Bailey's on top. I've had a stressful day."

"Because of the shop? I heard they found the guy. I'm just glad he didn't decide to hit me with something on his way out." Rarity sat back down and tore her bread stick in half. "Did you leave the door open? I've been trying to call you, but I guess you had your phone off since you were manning a table?"

"Yeah, I don't like to appear too busy to talk. I sold a lot of stuff over the last two days. I'll be back at the shop tomorrow, and like you, I'll get some locals who want an exclusive." She pushed her plate away. "Look, I've got to admit something."

"Okay." Rarity watched her friend. It was obvious that something was wrong. "Whatever it is, we'll get through it."

"I don't know. But look, I listened to the gossips in town, and I was mad at you for going after Drew." Sam exhaled like she'd been holding her breath. "There, I said it."

"I'm not 'going after Drew.' Why would I? We've talked about this." Rarity felt blindsided by Sam's accusation. "And I know you like him, so there's also that."

"I know. But he shows up here a lot." Sam waved her hand around the table. "With food."

"Which you're eating," Rarity reminded her friend. "Look. Drew and I are friends. We have some of the same interests. If he's interested in me romantically, I've made it plain that I am not interested in him that way. I just enjoy his company."

"I know. And I feel like a jerk. Especially after you risked your life going into my shop to check on me."

"Yes, I know. I am the better friend." Rarity laughed as Sam started to chuckle. "I'm just Saint Rarity."

"I wouldn't go that far, but thanks for dinner."

Rarity shrugged. "Don't thank me. Maybe you need to go check on Drew with a cup of coffee or something tonight and thank him."

"Sounds like a lot of work. Besides, I don't want him to get the idea that I'm okay with being at his beck and call all the time. Why don't we sit out on the deck with some wine after dessert and talk about something that doesn't involve Drew or his weird infatuation with you." Sam tried to hold her face serious but couldn't do it. She burst into giggles.

Rarity fake-flipped her hair off her shoulders. "There's nothing fake about the effect I have on all men. I have to beat them off with a stick, and Killer's been so busy biting ankles since I got him that his jaws are sore."

"Whatever." Sam laughed as she got up and put her plate in the sink. She threw away the empty food containers. "Where's this ice cream you promised?"

By the time Sam left to walk home, the bottle of wine they'd opened was empty, and the strain on their relationship was patched. Rarity had gotten out her notebook on Martha's murder and updated the information about Jonathon. Both Sam and Rarity agreed that if Jonathon was guilty of anything, it was of being too nice. He couldn't say no. They would update the Tuesday night group on what they'd found out.

Sam paused at the front door. "You know, maybe instead of getting our wires crossed by the gossips, we should use them. They knew about Jonathon and Martha. What else do they know that they aren't saying?"

"And what does Jonathon know that he doesn't realize is important?" Rarity added. "You're right, using the rumor mill wouldn't be a bad idea. We just need to find someone to pump for information."

"I think I have the exact right person. I'll call you tomorrow if it works out." Sam gave Rarity a hug.

"See you tomorrow." Rarity stayed on her porch and watched Sam walk down the sidewalk and toward town. She lived a few blocks over, but the subdivisions didn't match up so she couldn't just take a right at the next road. Sam had to go to Main Street, then walk over to her street, then walk back down the road to her house. Rarity wouldn't be able to see her for all that way, but she'd watch until she couldn't see her anymore.

"You've had a lot of visitors today." A voice came from the house next door to the left.

"Not really, just a couple of friends. I'm Rarity Cole. I own the bookstore downtown." She peered into the night and saw a man sitting in the dark on the deck.

"I know. I'm Terrance Oldman. Retired U.S. Navy." He walked over and leaned on the railing, where Rarity could see his face. "I know, why would a seaman retire in a desert? Let's just say I needed a change of scenery."

"Nice to meet you, Terrance. I knew people lived in the houses here, but I rarely see anyone." She crossed over to the edge of her front deck and leaned on the railing to match him.

"We've all become night owls. It's cool then, and we can hang out on our decks and watch. The problem is, not much happens here at night. We're all kind of boring." He chuckled.

"I like a boring neighborhood. It makes me feel safe." She thought about what he'd said. "So maybe I need to keep the shop open later at least one night a week. It would give you all a place to hang out."

"Sounds interesting. Let me talk with some of the others and see if they want to pull together a book club or a chess group or something to bring people in." He stood up straight. "Of course, it can't be too late for some. They have early bedtimes. We're a hard bunch to get together."

She said good night and realized Sam had already disappeared onto Main Street. She went inside and started turning off lights and cleaning up the kitchen. Whatever she'd said to Terrance, he'd been right. She'd had a lot of people over to her house today. More than since she'd been diagnosed and was going through treatment. But now, she didn't worry about what the house looked like or what she was going to serve.

Now it was just friends stopping by. And the good thing about friends was, they didn't care about what she wore or how her hair looked. They just wanted to talk to her.

It was a nice feeling.

Chapter 14

On Thursday, the walk to work didn't seem so long. Now that she'd met Terrance, she realized she was just on a different schedule than her neighbors. She no longer saw the place as creepy or abandoned. Just houses where people were probably sleeping or having breakfast as she walked to work.

As she turned onto Main Street, she saw a man on a bike moving down the empty street. He must be trying to get his exercise in before the day turned hot. She waved, and he waved back. Was that all it took to start to fit in? To be friendly herself?

She and Killer arrived at the bookstore, and she opened the door. Then she flipped over the CLOSED sign to OPEN and started opening the blinds in the shop. She booted up her laptop and saw an email from Drew.

Reading it, she almost didn't hear the bells go off over the door. Without looking up, she called out, "Welcome to The Next Chapter, I'll be right with you."

"If you're busy, I'll just drop this off. I stopped and got me one, so I thought you might like a coffee too." Sam walked toward the back and set the cup on the counter. "I'll see you later."

"No, hold up. I'm reading this email from Drew." When Sam didn't say anything, she looked up to see her friend glaring at her. "Stop, it's not like that. Anyway, he says they found a regular spa appointment in Martha's planner. He wants me to look at the website and see if it feels off."

"Feels off, like what?" Sam scooted closer to the screen.

Rarity turned it toward her and keyed in the website. When it came up, she nodded. "Drew was right. This isn't a normal spa. They're claiming the vortex it's located on has healing properties."

"It's not unusual for spas to 'claim' to have healing springs or rejuvenating powers." Sam shrugged. "What? I sell stones I believe help keep people well. What's the difference between gems and water?"

Rarity clicked on the "staff" tab and pointed to the man whose picture came up first. "You don't have a doctor saying your gems will cure people. Isn't this the guy that the medical people were talking about?"

"I don't remember hearing what his name was, do you?" Sam pulled out her phone and keyed a name into her search engine. "I'm getting the same website and not anything else. He's only attached to this spa and a line of creams."

Rarity pointed to the "products" tab. "Do you want to bet his products are made from the healing water?"

"We're in a desert. Any water we get out here is healing because we don't dry up." Sam nodded. "Let's see what he says."

It took her a while to go through the baskets that were for sale. You couldn't buy one just to try it out. All the products were bundled into a three- or six-month treatment plan. Rarity went to the "reservations" page. "Good—they have openings on Sunday. Do you want to go to a healing spa with me? I'll have to see if Drew can babysit Killer while we're gone, but it looks like we can get outpatient spa services that day if we sign up now."

Sam glanced at the prices. "I'm glad I had a good week selling, otherwise I couldn't afford even one of the treatments."

"I'll treat. We'll do the massage and the facial and attend the free anti-cancer diet plan meeting that afternoon. Then we'll drive back. I want to see what they might promise a woman who's scared the cancer might come back." Rarity signed up online and pulled out her credit card to pay for the reservation.

"Surely you don't think they'd talk about Martha if someone there killed her." Sam made a note in her phone. "I'll drive and buy gas. No arguing. You're spending a fortune as it is."

"I don't think they'll talk about Martha. I'm the one who's going to be the scared survivor. All you have to do is be my supportive friend. It's a role that works for you." Rarity opened Drew's email and wrote him a short note. His answer came back quicker than she'd expected.

Sam glanced over. "What did he say?"

"Well, he's going to watch Killer, but if we're even ten minutes late getting home, he's calling in the cavalry. He says it's dumb going in, but he won't stop us if we're careful." Rarity closed her laptop. "I guess we're going undercover. Maybe the police department will reimburse me the cost of the spa visit if we find something."

"One can only hope." Sam picked up her coffee. "I've got to get to work. I've got a ton of receipts to go through and log the email addresses into my newsletter contact list."

"You have a newsletter for your shop?" Rarity called after her.

"You don't?" Sam shook her head. "We'll talk marketing on the way to the spa. There's so much you need to learn. Bye, Killer."

Killer barked as Sam left the building. He was becoming more and more social, which made her think the decision to bring him to the bookstore while she worked had been a good one. She opened her laptop again and started to research current books on the fake cancer cure industry. She found a few books, but mostly it was articles that she found on the internet.

With the shop slow, she was able to get through several of the articles and found more references, which did include additional books to read.

"It's like doing a research paper," Rarity said to Killer as they ate a small lunch at the fireplace. She left the store open, just in case someone came in, but they were able to eat their lunch in peace. She'd only had three customers so far that day—five if you counted Sam and the delivery guy from the café who had brought her a turkey sandwich on multigrain bread. She looked through the notes she'd made as she'd researched. She'd ordered five more books this morning just to see if they had anything she could use in helping Drew solve Martha's murder. But she doubted it.

The best way to stop people from being taken by scams like this spa they were visiting on Sunday was to give them access to reading material that demonstrated what was real and what wasn't. She wouldn't have time to read all the books before her spa appointment, but she'd start one as soon as the book order came in tomorrow.

Owning a bookstore had its perks, even if she'd had to pay extra to add the books to her order this week.

* * * *

By the time Sam showed up at her house on Sunday morning, Rarity had done a lot of research on the power of the local waters for healing. There were places in the area called vortexes, and many of the spas focused on the spiritual healing that could be found at such places. Live Long and Prevention was the only resort in the area claiming to have a medical doctor on staff, as well as programs to heal such problems as diabetes, fibromyalgia, and most cancers. According to the website, cancer was caused due to a stress fissure in the body that never healed. Rarity read

Sam some highlights she'd found on the resort's website. "Relationship issues are the number-one cause of cancer cells growing out of control."

"Well, now we know that Kevin not only refused to deal with your illness, he also caused it. I told you that boy was no good for you." Sam turned her SUV onto the main highway. "I thought maybe I'd see Drew when I picked you up?"

"He came by at six and grabbed Killer and his toys. He's working today, so he wanted to get Killer settled at the house before he left. I guess Jonathon and Edith are going into Phoenix for the day." Rarity plugged the address to the resort into Sam's phone so the GPS would show on her car's display. "He'll be at the house when we get back. He's grilling dinner for us."

"Really?" Sam shot a glance at Rarity. "You gave him the key to your house?"

"He's a police detective. What's going to happen?" She shook her head and went back to her tablet, where she had pulled the website up. "According to this, the entire resort and product line is overseen by a Dr. Conrad. No first name, so maybe his folks named him 'Doctor,' just in case he couldn't get into medical school."

"Very funny. I wish you would have told me that Drew was going to be at your house later. I would have worn something different." She rubbed the leg of her yoga pants.

"I don't think it's a date. I think he's using my empty house to get some time away from his folks. They're driving him crazy." Rarity tapped the tablet. "They have a picture of the doctor, but no pictures of other staff. Do you think that's odd?"

"Maybe he likes the attention. Most doctors do." Sam passed a Jeep with a couple of tourists obviously looking for a road or a sign to a trailhead. "Do you really think this place has something to do with what happened to Martha?"

Rarity set the tablet down. She'd gone over the website pages time and time again to find some sort of clue that she could give Drew with a 'that's how you solve a case' flourish. The problem was that so far, she hadn't found anything that seemed out of the ordinary except for the place's claims to heal things that in her mind weren't healable. At least not by diet and exercise and thinking good thoughts. "They should call it the Tinkerbell Resort. All we have to do is believe that our cancer is gone, and *poof*, it will magically disappear."

"I didn't know Martha well, but she doesn't seem the type to just believe in the positive. In fact, the only thing positive about Martha was the way she dealt with Killer." Sam turned off the highway and onto a side road. "Ten more miles, and we'll be there."

"I wonder when Martha got Killer? Maybe he was her gateway drug into all things positive. Having a dog makes you a more agreeable person. At least, that's the thought process." Rarity pulled a notebook out of her purse. "I'll ask the vet if they can tell me how old Killer is. If Martha got him as a puppy, that might be when she started believing all this stuff."

"And you need to know how old Killer is for his medical records." Sam slowed the car as the speed limit dropped. "You're good at this investigation thing."

"Only in some ways. All I seem to do is be able to prove that each of our 'suspects' didn't kill Martha. I haven't been able to find anyone who did, who had motive, opportunity, and means." Rarity watched out the window and saw a hawk dive for something on the desert floor. Probably a mouse. Mice were always the easy prey of the animal kingdom. "Anyway, if you're worried about how you look, you can borrow something from my room. I've got several sundresses that would look ultra-cute on you."

"I just need to get over the fear this man puts into my head. Every time I think about talking to Drew, my mouth dries up and my heart starts beating faster. Maybe I'm just being silly even thinking about dating him." She focused on the road instead of meeting Rarity's gaze. "And you and him are becoming good friends. Which is cool, but it makes me worry that I will never be truly comfortable with him. Not like you are."

"I feel that way about Archer." Rarity shook her head. "I know I said I wasn't interested in him, but he walks into my shop and I'm all tongue-tied. Thank goodness we have something to talk about with the hiking books. At least that keeps me from looking like a complete idiot."

Sam laughed, and her grip on the steering wheel eased a bit. "Look at the two of us acting like schoolkids. Let's just change the subject. I want to have a story to tell the group on Tuesday when we meet. What are we looking for? Do we have a backstory for the spa about how we know Martha?"

"Let's just keep it simple and real. We met Martha at our book club, and she mentioned the resort and how much it had helped her. Since I have a history of breast cancer, I am looking for a way to make sure it doesn't come back again." Rarity closed the tablet and tucked it into her tote.

"And I'm your faithful friend who would walk with you to the ends of the earth to help keep you healthy." Sam pushed her hair behind her ears. "I can play that. Although I'm much better in lead roles than I am being a supportive cast member."

"Next time you can be the leading lady." Rarity turned up the music. "I really love this song."

* * * *

When they got to the resort, a valet took the car and handed Sam a ticket, which she tucked into her wallet. They walked under the pergolas and into the open-area lobby. A fountain was bubbling in the middle of the room, and the ceiling was three stories high. The rooms all faced out onto the courtyard in the middle of the lobby. A man in a polo shirt and chino pants approached.

"May I help you, ladies?" He bowed a bit. "Do you need directions to the hotel front desk, the spa receiving area, or just the gift shop?"

Rarity and Sam exchanged a glance, which meant they both thought the place was trying way too hard. "We've got some treatments scheduled for today. I'm afraid this is our first time here, so we're a little lost."

"But I love the idea of a gift shop. How late is it open?" Sam asked. She'd upped the chirpiness of her voice two octaves. It was almost high enough to call a pack of dogs to do her bidding.

"Ten p.m. And it reopens at six in the morning. Seven days a week." He pointed toward the left corner of the lobby. "Just go down that hallway, and you'll find it. But the spa is on the opposite side of the lobby. Let me show you."

They followed the man to the edge of the lobby and into a small arched hallway. He paused at the beginning of the area. "Male staffers aren't allowed past this line, I'm afraid. If you just head straight down the hallway, you'll find the spa desk. Emerald will be glad to help you get set up."

He turned and left them. Rarity held out her hand. "After you."

"Oh no, I insist. I'm just the supportive cast member, remember?"

Rarity laughed and headed down the dark hallway. It was a bit creepy. She wondered why male staff weren't allowed in the area, but as soon as they stepped into the lights of the reception room, she had her answer.

Women were walking around in all stages of dress—from fully clothed to totally disrobed. Big, tall, skinny, fat, all colors and all ages, it didn't seem to matter. These women were comfortable in their own skin. A waitress in a white uniform with a tray of refreshing drinks paused near them.

"Cucumber-lime water?" the waitress asked.

Sam took two glasses and handed one to Rarity. "Where do we check in?"

The woman nodded toward the front of the room. "Vi will get you checked in and to your appointment. We're busy today. Usually, the front area isn't so"—she paused and looked around the room—"crowded."

"Thanks." Sam sipped her water as they walked toward the desk, where the woman who must be Vi was now watching them.

Rarity wondered if the waitress had somehow alerted the woman that there were new people in the room. "The curtain just went up on our performance. Get as much as you can."

"Okay, but I think Holly and Malia are going to want to come check out this place too. Just in case we missed something." Sam grinned as she followed Rarity to the desk.

"Good morning, I'm so glad you could make it today. Can I get your names so I can get you checked in and we can start your experience?" Vi bubbled energy, even around the mundane part of check-in.

After giving their names, Rarity looked around, wide-eyed. "Wow, I didn't think it would be like this. Our friend Martha, she's the one who recommended it, and she was a little conservative."

Vi giggled. "You came on the first Sunday of the month. We host a local naturalist colony then. They are very comfortable here—and very good tippers."

"Oh, that explains it. Martha, is—I mean, *was*—a very private person. This didn't seem to be her scene."

Vi's face fell. "Oh no. I didn't put it together. You're friends of Martha Redding. The woman they just found out by the trail. It's so sad. She was such a nice woman. I helped with her mud baths once a week, and we talked about our dogs. She loved her little dog."

"Killer. He's with me now." Rarity took a sip of the cucumber-lime water. "I guess if one good thing came out of Martha's death, it was me getting that little fur ball. He's so sweet. I can't believe you can fall in love so fast with anything."

Vi stood and pulled out several clipboards with forms attached. "Let's go to the massage waiting room. You can fill out your paperwork there. It's a little more private. I have a Maltese named Pepper. I don't know what I'd do without him. He's my little man."

Vi continued to tell stories about Pepper and his misdeeds as they walked down the hall to the massage area. They passed by an office with large glass windows. A man stood at the door, watching them pass by.

Chapter 15

Sam squeaked a little, and Rarity and Vi glanced back at her. Vi stepped back and took Sam's arm, hurrying her past the window. Vi shushed her as they moved past the office. "That's Dr. Conrad. He likes to keep an eye on things."

Rarity paused by the doorway and watched as the doctor turned and spoke to the woman who sat at the reception desk. He glanced their way, then disappeared through a doorway into what must have been another office. She saw his name painted on the glass door. "I didn't realize Dr. Conrad had his offices in this part of the building. The man who helped us find you said no men were allowed in the area."

"No male staff members. Dr. Conrad and his assistants are the only men allowed back here. Of course, Dr. Conrad is the only one of them who works on Sundays. I swear, that man is so dedicated to the clinic. He really needs to learn to take some personal time." Vi opened the door and waved them into the massage area. "You'll start here, and I'll come back for your paperwork in a few minutes. There are drinks in the fridge, help yourself."

After Vi left, Sam sank into a chair. "Is there anything with some caffeine in there? Seeing him standing there, watching us, it was creepy."

"I know. I'm not sure what's all going on here, but it seems a little off." Rarity sorted through the sodas in the small fridge. "Sorry, nothing with any caffeine, but there's some root beer."

"That will have to do." Sam opened the can and took a sip of the soda, glancing around the room. "Investigating is hard work. I have a lot more respect for Drew's profession right about now."

Rarity leaned close and whispered, "Shush. You don't know if they have cameras in here."

Sam rolled her eyes and started filling out the paperwork. "You think of everything. Looking at possible options for our next visit, I'm not sure I want a colonic, even if it comes with a full package."

Rarity got the giggles, and it wasn't until the attendant came into the room that she was able to stop.

"Good morning. My name is Ingrid. Who's up for a massage?" the young woman asked as she held out two robes. "We have two slots open right now. We've just cleaned the rooms, so they're all sanitized, and as soon as you change into your robes, we can begin. There's a changing room behind that door, and you can leave your paperwork here in the room. Vi will come back for it."

Rarity signed the last page and stood. "I'm so stressed out, I need two massages."

"Oh no. Well, we only allow one a day, but maybe you could come back for one of our retreats. You can see Dr. Conrad, and he'll help you deal with that stress." Ingrid looked pained to have to give Rarity the bad news.

"Oh, Ingrid, I wish it was that simple. One of our friends died the other day, and it's just been crazy ever since. I can't help thinking that I could have done more to help." Rarity bit her lower lip, hoping she looked like she was grieving.

"I know exactly how you feel. We're not supposed to talk about it to our guests, but it's such a coincidence. One of our long-term patients was killed in Sedona last week. It's heartbreaking." She frowned as she glanced between Sam and Rarity. "Wait, you're not talking about Martha, are you?"

Rarity nodded, wiping away a fake tear. "She was part of our book club. In fact, she recommended this place to us."

"Martha was a lovely person. Very concerned about her health after her cancer came back." Ingrid took a deep breath. "I may not be able to get you more than one massage today, but I'll add on a hot stone treatment to the package you bought. And you'll still be done before it's time for your lunch. Then, after lunch, you'll soak in the hot spring water. It's actually from a local spring—we heat it here, but it is a local spring near a vortex. You'll be feeling better before you leave today, I promise."

Sam stood and set down her soda. "So, I guess it's time to get changed, then. I didn't know Martha's cancer had returned. Did you, Rarity?"

"I knew she was a survivor, like me." Rarity loved the way Sam put information out there for Ingrid to respond to.

"She came for a treatment about a year ago, and Dr. Conrad found the recurrence when he reviewed her paperwork. She's very lucky he's so good at his job." Ingrid picked up their soda cans and dumped the rest into a sink nearby. "Go ahead and put on the robes, and we'll get your own life-changing experiences started."

Rarity and Sam went into the changing room. Rarity checked to see if it was empty, then stood close to Sam. "Help me get this jacket unzipped, will you? It always sticks."

Sam reached up and pretended to struggle with the jacket. She turned her face down and away and whispered, "I'm smelling a rat."

"Just keep your eyes open. We don't know whether this place had anything to do with her death." Rarity smiled and raised her voice. "Thank you for the help. I don't know why I don't just get a new jacket."

"Besides the fact that you're cheap?" Sam offered with a grin.

"I paid for your spa day, so I'm not *so* cheap," Rarity teased back.

As soon as they'd changed, another attendant entered the room. "Good, you're ready. Come this way."

Sam and Rarity shared a look. If they weren't watching them on monitors, they had the changing process timed to a science. Rarity went into the first room, and Sam was led to the next room.

After their massages, lunch was served in a small dining room with other participants, all of whom were all wearing robes. The food was mostly vegetable-based, and there was a flyer given to each diner on the need for more nutrients in their food—as well as a list of supplements available for purchase at the gift shop on their way out.

Sam ate her salad, poking through the lettuce to try to find the slivers of almonds and cranberries. "We should stop by the drive-in on the way home. I'm going to be starving by the time we leave here."

"I don't know. I'm enjoying my meal." Rarity kicked Sam under the table to remind her they were probably still being watched. "Maybe we should come back for the detox. Five days like this, and I bet I'd lose twenty pounds."

"I'm betting five at the most." Sam sighed as she focused on the flyer next to her. She pointed to the description of the detox. "See here, they only guarantee three pounds. And that's probably all water weight."

"At least it's a start," Rarity protested, then went on to change the subject. She didn't know if this was telling her anything about Martha, except that the woman really liked to take care of herself. Something Rarity wouldn't have guessed from the one and only book club meeting Martha had attended.

By the time they left that night, they had sat through a thirty-minute presentation on the other offerings the spa had and had walked through the gift shop. Sam made up an excuse for them to get out of there without buying anything. Driving home, Sam rolled her shoulders. "It was a great spa, but they're so focused on the hard sell. This will help your skin, it's looking a little muddy, don't you think?"

"I thought you were going to punch her when she told you your lips were chapped, and you needed to buy their salve before your next date." Rarity yawned and settled into the seat. "And they brought up the detox. I told you those waiters refilling our water glasses every five minutes were listening to our conversation. It's probably all in our file. I bet I'll get a sales call tomorrow morning."

"Do you want tacos? The stand just after the turnoff is pretty good."

Rarity nodded. "That sounds awesome. Just a couple, though, since Drew's grilling dinner for us."

"I'd forgotten about that. Okay, so how about one each and a soda. I need some caffeine." Sam pulled up to the order window.

"Get me two. I'm starving. And hard-shell tacos aren't very big. And a Coke." Rarity pulled out her credit card, but Sam waved it away.

"I'll get this." Sam called their order into the speaker and took some cash out of her center console. "So our first sleuthing adventure was successful."

"How do you figure that? We don't have anything to tell Drew or the book club on Tuesday." Rarity stared out the side window and thought she saw Ingrid and Vi getting out of a car and walking into the taco stand.

"Don't be so sure. Checking out something and finding out there's nothing there makes one less spot that Drew has to focus on." Sam moved the car up in line. "I love a good drive-thru."

"Look over there. Are those our friends from the spa?" Rarity guessed Sam's theory was true, but it seemed like a waste of time. It would have been a great spa day, if the staff hadn't been so focused on selling the next treatment.

"I guess the staff doesn't all just eat salads and sprouts." Sam laughed as the woman at the window took her money.

The woman glanced toward where Sam was looking. "I take it you've been to the spa?"

"You get a lot of business from them, I take it?" Sam held her hand out for the change.

"You wouldn't believe how much. We can always tell when a session's let out, since we get slammed. And their employees eat here too." She handed Sam a bag. "Our food's twice as good. And still healthy for you."

As they drove away, Sam sipped on her soda. "I'm not sure about the tacos being healthy, but I'm enjoying the sugar in this soda."

"Do you want to stop at the overlook and eat so you won't have shell crumbs all over yourself when we see Drew?" Rarity asked.

Sam smiled at her. "You're a great friend, you know that, right?"

* * * *

When they got back to the house, she spied Drew outside on the deck talking to another man. Rarity could only see the guy's back from the doorway. Great, a double date setup. Rarity scooped up a barking Killer and gave him a hug as she opened the sliding glass door and stepped out on the deck. And right into Archer. She felt her cheeks flush as she managed an "Oh, hi."

"Hey, you're back. And still alive. I was worried. I've never sent civilians undercover into an investigation before." Drew opened the cooler. "I have beer on ice for your trouble."

"Don't tell me you don't want our very thorough report before we start drinking. Oh, wait, you already checked the place out and were just humoring us." Rarity took the beer he offered her. "I see how it is. Hi, Archer. I didn't know you knew our scheming police detective here."

"Actually, Drew and I went to school together. We've been friends for a while." He reached out to pet Killer. "I didn't know you two were acquainted, though."

"Barely. He likes my dog, so I let him hang around here sometimes." She nodded toward Sam. "You remember my friend Sam?"

"You two are some of my best local customers." He tipped his beer bottle toward her. "Nice to see you again."

"Nice to see you too." Sam focused on Drew. "So you'd already talked to the spa people about Martha? Don't you think the place is a little off? It gave me goosebumps at times."

"I do want your impressions. That's why I sent you there. So are you saying 'off,' as in focused on the buck rather than the healing they claim to do? Definitely. I think they were robbing Martha blind with all those supplements and food shakes. Remember I've been in her house. They were all over the place." Drew went back to the grill and opened it. "Now, I like to get my nutrients the old-fashioned way. I hope you all like steaks."

"Works for me," Sam said, shooting a glance at Rarity.

"Sorry, I'm off most red meats. Just a taste thing after the chemo. I've got a chicken breast in the fridge if you wouldn't mind grilling that. I'll go grab and season it." She moved toward the kitchen.

When she returned, he took the plate from her and opened the grill. "I'm the one who should be sorry. I didn't even think. I should have asked this morning."

"No need to be worried about it. I see you all brought a variety of salads and fruits and vegetable trays for snacking. I wouldn't have gone hungry." She took the now-empty plate.

"Yeah, but I should have been more thoughtful." He glanced at his watch. "We'll be ready to eat in about fifteen, twenty minutes. Do you want to eat out here by the pool?"

"Sounds perfect." She took the plate back in the kitchen and was surprised when Archer followed her. "I'm glad Drew dragged you along."

"I'm glad you're glad. He said it would be cool with you, but I just want to make sure. If it's weird somehow, I'll eat and leave." He met her gaze and held it.

She couldn't catch her breath. Finally, she reached for the cabinet and started loading up a tray with flatware, napkins, plates, and seasonings. She waited until she'd felt her face cool a bit before turning around. "Why would it be weird? I enjoy your company. Do you want to help me get stuff outside so we can get the table set up?"

"I'm here to serve." He smiled, and as he picked up the tray she'd just filled, she noticed the dimples in his cheeks. He paused at the sliding door. "Are you coming?"

"I'll be right out. I've got to grab something." She hurried into her bedroom and the en suite bath and closed the door. Then she ran cold water over her hands, letting the chill bring her temperature down and slow her heart rate. She studied her face in the mirror. "He's just here as Drew's friend. Stop pretending you're in a regency romance."

She wasn't sure either she or the woman in the mirror believed her words. But she dried her hands and then went to set out the salads that Drew and Archer had brought over for dinner. One thing was certain, they wouldn't starve. Even if they were stuck in the house for the next week.

As they were eating, Drew's phone buzzed. He picked it up, read the text, then set it back down.

"Something important?" Sam asked.

He shrugged. "The coroner just got back to me on a question I had. Nothing I need to handle right now."

Rarity studied him, thinking about the day they'd had at the health spa. Something had bothered her when they'd been talking with Vi and Ingrid. Now she couldn't put her finger on it. It hadn't been a lie, but it had been something surprising. Now she couldn't remember what it had been.

He shook his head. "Don't even ask because I'm not going to tell you. You and Sam did enough by going to the spa. Send me your receipt, and I'll get your expenses reimbursed. I appreciate your insight."

"Did you talk with Kelly O'Reilly yet?" Sam surprised Rarity by pushing the subject.

"He has an alibi for the night Martha died. And yes, he was seeing both Martha and Gay at the same time. That's not a crime." Drew cut his steak and took a bite. "Everything tastes better grilled."

"Not everything. Chocolate doesn't taste better grilled," Archer challenged him. "Who's Gay?"

"Gay is Madame Zelda's real name. We went to school with her daughter, Heather. Don't you remember?" He cut another slice of steak and ate it.

"No way. Skinny kid, glasses, always had her nose in a book?" He smiled at Rarity. "No offense to our local bookseller here."

"That's her. Heather and I dated for a while, then she went off to college and met someone in computers. Gay told me she thought her daughter was an idiot leaving me behind. That I was the only guy Heather dated that she could even stand." He picked up the potato salad container and refilled his plate. Then he handed the container to Archer.

"Wait a minute. I dated Heather sophomore year." He set the container down without taking anything.

Rarity and Sam locked gazes and broke out into giggles. Finally, Sam came up for air. "I'm not sure if that was true or not, but the two of you are hilarious."

"So, you don't think Kelly had anything to do with Martha's death?" Rarity played with a piece of watermelon on her plate. "I've handed you two suspects on a platter, and you've managed to alibi them both out. I'm beginning to think you're not trying very hard."

"Honestly, I want to get this case off my desk. I'm tired of people showing up telling me about the time they saw Martha talking to one random person or another." He set his fork down. "I know people want to help, but all I'm getting are vague descriptions, which I'm thinking are mostly sightings of her and Kelly."

"I think they're just trying to help, Drew." Archer grabbed one of the cookies off a plate in the middle of the table. "I hear about the murder all the time on the hikes. I'm worried it's going to affect the tourist trade."

"I've heard that from the business chamber too." Drew stood and walked over to the pool, then knelt beside it. He ran his hand in the water. "Everyone needs Martha's killer brought to justice."

Chapter 16

On Monday morning, Rarity headed outside to her pool to do laps before starting her day. She wasn't opening the bookstore this morning. No conventions were in town, so it wasn't worth the time. Besides, she knew she needed time off from the job, even if it was becoming her life. Before she'd been diagnosed, she was a self-proclaimed workaholic. She loved the fast-paced run she'd maintained to be at the top of her game. It didn't matter who the client was, she was their number-one fan, at least until their contract was over. She logged sixty- to seventy-hour workweeks during most campaigns. Looking back on it now, she wondered if she'd worked herself into the cancer diagnosis. Her body's way of waving a white flag and giving up.

Now she swore she was going to be more focused on healthy living. Like making sure she took time for exercise. Once she'd paid the extra money to get the house with the pool, she felt duty-bound to use it.

She floated in the cool water for a bit, thinking about how enjoyable last night had been. She hoped she could stay friends with Drew and Archer, no matter what happened in the love department. She'd enjoyed dinner and their game of cards afterward. She hadn't played blackjack in forever. Starting with a soft side stroke, she focused on her swim and the memories playing in her head.

She made the turn for the last few laps and looked up to see someone watching her from the deck. She blinked the water out of her eyes and saw Drew standing at the end of the pool. He was holding out her towel. She walked through the water toward him. "I take it my swim's over?"

"I've got a couple of questions you might be able to answer for me, if you have a minute." He jerked his head toward the house. "Do you have coffee made?"

"I have a Keurig. Make me a cup while you're in there, and I'll finish off my laps for the day." She leaned back and started the backstroke for her last five laps. Then she stepped out of the pool, drying off with the towel he'd left on a chair by the stairs. She didn't wear a swim cap, so she dried her hair first, then wrapped the towel around herself and went to the table to wait.

He brought out two steaming cups of coffee and set one before her. "Sorry to bother you this early, but something's bothering me."

"About the medical examiner's report." Rarity could see by his face that she'd hit the nail on the head.

"Yeah." He sipped his coffee. "Martha didn't have a relapse or a recurrence of cancer. The tox report didn't show any cancer medications in her blood work. So, why was she going to that spa for cancer treatments?"

"That's what was bothering me, too. I was told by several people, including workers at the spa, that she'd just beaten cancer again. And so it wasn't fair that she was killed." She sipped her coffee. "It could be the spa's doctor is just a modern traveling medicine man with a new twist."

"But would that be enough for someone to kill her over?" He shook his head. "That spa has tons of reviews saying that people questioned their medical advice, but the massages were supposedly top-notch."

"If Martha threatened to expose them, they'd probably laugh in her face. There are plenty of places selling get-healthy-quick scams. Just think about all the weight-loss miracle cures you can find on the internet." Rarity finished his thought for him.

Killer barked at her feet. She picked up the little dog, and he cuddled into her towel. Rarity rubbed his ears.

"I wish Killer could talk. Maybe he'd give us some clues to solve this murder."

Drew finished off his coffee. "Thanks for talking that out with me. I didn't mean to interrupt your swim."

"I was glad to help. When you got the text last night, I knew something was off with the results. I just wish I could be more helpful."

"You and Sam have done a lot. I appreciate the leads you've brought my way. And that you have kept from investigating yourselves. I'd hate to have to throw one of you in jail for obstruction." He put on his ball cap and rubbed Killer's head on the way out through the gate. "You might want to put a lock on your gate. I got in here way too easily."

"Says the man who just broke into my backyard."

He paused at the gate. "I thought I heard someone calling for help and splashing. It was an urgent situation."

"Whatever, go to work." She stood and took his cup inside along with her own. She had some house chores to do, but first, she was going to shower and change. Then it was time to finish that mystery she'd gotten as an ARC last week from a publisher. It had been over a year since the author's last book, and she'd been excited to get a chance to read his new one.

A knock on the front door made her turn back from the hallway. Drew must have forgotten something.

She swung open the door to see Terrance, her neighbor, standing there. "Oh, good morning. What can I do for you?"

"I was just checking to see if everything was all right." He glanced around her into the living room. "No one is bothering you, are they?"

"I'm sorry?" Rarity was totally confused by the line of conversation.

"I just meant, with the police being here, I was hoping that there was nothing happening. I guess I just let my imagination run wild. I'm not much for calling the police." He shuffled from one foot to the other.

"No worries. Drew was just here talking about our dinner party last night. I'm sorry if seeing his cruiser worried you."

Terrance laughed. "I guess having a neighbor who's good friends with the law isn't the worst thing you could ask for. Sorry I bothered you."

"You didn't bother me. I like seeing you. For a while, I didn't think I had any neighbors at all." She shut the door and thought about what Terrance had told her. People weren't as closed off here as she'd originally thought. It was shaping up to be a good day.

* * * *

On Tuesday night, the group came at six and shared food before even looking at the clock. Everyone was there except for Kim. She glanced around the group. "Does anyone know where Kim's at? Should we wait a few more minutes? And who made the mint brownies? They're delicious."

Malia raised her hand. "The brownies are mine. I'm so glad you like them. I haven't heard from Kim. Maybe she had a treatment, and she's sick?"

Shirley shook her head. "Kim called just as I was packing up to come. She said that things were bad at work and she couldn't make it tonight. But if we choose another book, she wanted us to let her know."

"Do we want to talk about the book or Martha's murder?" Rarity asked.

Quickly, the answers came flying back. Talking about Martha had won.

"Okay, let's go over anything new anyone found out this week." She turned the page on the flipchart to a blank page.

"Kelly O'Reilly is hurting for money. He's been getting advances from the bank on his upcoming contracts," Shirley said as she crocheted on her blanket.

"How did you find that out?" Rarity wrote the bit of info down.

Shirley looked up after finishing a row and turning it to the next one. "One of my best friends works at the bank. I know she's not supposed to tell people things like that, but we went out for a few drinks last week, and I asked her if she knew him. Boy, did I get an earful."

Rarity let Shirley tell her story, but Drew's admission that Kelly had an alibi kept ringing in her head.

"He's always been on the edge with his deals, but lately he's been missing his deadlines. Not enough to where they have to resort to legal proceedings, but close." Shirley set her crochet hook down. "And I've seen Martha's house. She's got some land around her, and she's close enough to town that he'd be able to sell it for a bunch if he found the right investors."

"Sounds like motive to me. He wines and dines her until she changes her will, then kills her off." Holly pulled out a notebook. "I should have thought of this before. I'll check the status of Martha's property and see who is listed on the deed. If she owned it free and clear, it makes the motive even more solid."

"Except Kelly has an alibi for the time Martha was killed. As does our friend Madame Zelda." Rarity wrote the word *alibi* by each of their names, then wrote two questions on the page. Pointing to the first question, the one about the property, she nodded to Holly. "I think you're right about checking the deed. That gives us more information. And we need to see if Martha left a will."

Malia raised her hand. "There's only one lawyer in town, so if she used him, he's my uncle. I'll go over and chat up his secretary and see what I can find out. If she went to Flagstaff, though, we're going to be out of luck."

"Okay, then." Rarity wrote Holly and Malia's names by the questions. "Now, Sam and I have a report. I think we were sent on a royal goose chase by Drew Anderson, but here's what we found out."

She went on to tell them all about their spa day and what they'd learned from the staff members. "Drew confirmed that Martha had bought tons of their products. And the staff members at this spa think their doctor is some kind of medical god. So, they're very convincing when they talk about their products and services."

"Except we found out that most of them still eat fast food. At least they like tacos," Rarity added.

"Yeah, we found them at the closest drive-thru to the spa, eating real food, like normal people." Sam laughed at the memory. "So, they aren't as all-in as they appear when they're at work."

"I wonder if we could use that somehow?" Rarity put a question mark by Ingrid and Vi's names.

"If you need someone to go back to the spa and ask, Malia and I will go." Holly raised her hand excitedly.

Rarity looked at Sam. "I told you they'd be questioning our investigative techniques."

"Not your skills, but maybe wondering why you're getting the primo assignments. Although it was a good idea to go out there." Holly stood and got another brownie. "Another week gone, and we're out of suspects."

Rarity sat down and reviewed the murder board, as they'd begun to call it. "Maybe. But I'm thinking there's still a few questions we don't have answered. Like, who gets Martha's money? If it's her best friend from years ago, Madame Zelda, maybe she has an alibi, but she used someone else to do the deed." She paused for a moment. "I think we're looking at this wrong."

"What do you mean?" Shirley had opened her notebook and was writing down the new information.

"We're looking at who might have killed Martha, but not the why. Why would someone kill her? I think if we answer that question, the murderer will become obvious." Rarity took another brownie off the plate that Holly was passing around.

The clock chimed nine, and Shirley stood up. "I've got to get home. George worries when I'm later than normal. I'll talk to some people at church and see if anyone knows who Martha's heirs were. Malia's uncle gave a talk a few years ago about preparing our wills. I wasn't there since George and I have had our wills for years, but I think I remember Martha attending."

"I'll try to track down Vi and Ingrid from the spa. They both said they had dogs and talked to Martha a lot about them. Maybe I can use the 'I need to find her vet' approach." Rarity glanced over at Killer, who was still asleep on his bed by the fireplace. "And I have a real vet appointment for him this week anyway, so I'll see if anyone there knew her."

"For being such a grump, she sure did talk to a lot of different people about Killer." Sam stood and grabbed a trash bag from the counter by the register.

"Pets bring out the best in us," Shirley said as she walked toward the doorway. "I'll see you all next Tuesday. I'm having so much fun."

Soon everyone had left besides Sam. "Let me clean out the coffeepot for you."

Rarity went over and locked the door, turning the sign to *closed*. "Sounds good. I'll grab the rest of the lemonade."

"We're close to figuring this out, I can feel it." Sam waited for Rarity to pick up the pitcher before heading back to the small kitchenette in the back of the building. "Everyone is so involved in finding information."

Rarity sighed as she found an empty bottle to pour the leftover lemonade into. "That's what worries me. What if the killer figures out what we're doing? What if he or she comes after one of the girls? Or Shirley?"

"Or one of us? Remember? We're doing the investigation stuff too. In fact, we went to that creepy spa on Sunday." Sam dumped the leftover coffee and washed the pot and the coffee filter holder.

"Yeah, but we know what we're doing."

"And you're saying the others don't? Wow, don't let Shirley hear you say that." Sam set the pot and filter on the plastic drainer by the sink. "Look, I know you're worried about this. But we're all adults. We know what we're getting ourselves into. And, as far as Holly and Malia go, I think it's good to have the group to keep them out of trouble. If the two of them went off on their own and didn't think they had to answer to the book club, they might have Kelly O'Reilly tied up in some basement trying to sweat the truth out of him."

Rarity laughed as she put the drink into the fridge and changed places with Sam so she could wash the glass pitcher. "You're right, of course. We're a mediating factor for those two. But they're smart and a little impulsive. Malia found the car before we even knew Martha was dead."

"True, but she talks to a lot of people. I'm don't know what her job is, but she seems to know everyone in town."

Killer barked from the doorway of the kitchen.

"And there's our alarm clock. He says it's time to go home and snuggle up in bed after he gets his treat." Rarity fed him at the shop on Tuesday since they got home so much later due to the book club. "Are you going home or heading out?"

"Home. Drew said to call him when I got home and maybe he'd come over for a while." Sam grinned. "I cleaned house all day yesterday just on a maybe he might be showing up. At least the public parts. I'm going to lead him out to the deck so he doesn't see the dust in the television room. I didn't get that cleaned."

"I think a couple of hours on the deck would be lovely." Rarity made shooing movements with her hand. "Go on, I'm going to dump this trash in the dumpster, then I'll be out of here too."

"I'll wait until you're back inside, then you can walk out with me. I'll feel better. You remember someone was hanging out back when they broke into my shop," Sam reminded her.

"Technically, they didn't break in, but I get what you're saying. I'll be right back." Rarity grabbed the two trash bags and went out the back door into the alley. The moonlight was just beginning to make the world bright, but the area had streetlights that lined the back area where the alley touched the open desert. She didn't see anything or anyone out of place, but a shiver went down her spine anyway. She paused at the steps, listening. But all she heard was the occasional car going past on Main Street and the faint sound of the patrons enjoying the country music at the Garnet.

She hurried over and tucked the sacks into the dumpster she shared with the rest of the businesses nearby. As she stepped away, she almost tripped over a box that was lying near the dumpster. She picked it up and realized it was filled with bottles of what sounded like pills. She took it inside, wondering if someone had set it down when they'd dropped off the trash and forgotten to pick it back up.

"What's that?" Sam asked as she watched Rarity come back inside.

"Someone left this box out by the dumpster. I wanted to check and make sure it wasn't by mistake, since the trash pickup is tomorrow." She took a knife and opened the seal. Bottles and containers of salves and supplements were in the box. She held one up for Sam to see. "These are from the spa."

"Who were they sent to?" Sam asked as Rarity turned the box lip back down so she could see the shipping label.

She read it and then looked up at Sam. "Madame Zelda."

Chapter 17

Instead of Drew meeting Sam at her house, he said he would come to the bookstore after Sam called him and told him about the box of spa items they'd found. Rarity thought about making more coffee as they waited, but decided against it. If she drank any more, she'd never get to sleep. She and Sam sat near the fireplace and waited for Drew to arrive.

Killer lay in Rarity's lap. Every once in a while, he'd raise his head with a look on his face that said he was wondering when they were going home, but then she'd just pet him and he'd settle again.

Finally, Drew arrived, and when Rarity opened the door for him, she realized he had Archer in tow as well. She held the door open wider. "I didn't think it took two of you to pick up a box."

"Archer's driving you and Killer home. I'll take Sam home, but I have to drop this box off at the station first." Drew stepped inside and looked around. "Where did you leave it?"

"It's on the coffee table." Rarity pointed to the fireplace area. Then she shut the door after Archer. "I'm sorry he dragged you down here. I can walk home by myself."

"No problem. Besides, if Drew's concerned, so am I. I was just watching reruns of *Gilligan's Island* anyway. I love that show." Archer nodded to the fireplace area. "Should we go join the others?"

When they got there, Drew had his camera out and was taking pictures of the box. "Where did you find this?"

"Out by the dumpster. I brought it in so it wouldn't be picked up in the morning when the trash came. The sanitation guys are really good about cleaning up around the dumpsters when they come by. So, if someone had just forgotten it, it would have been gone when they went back."

"Or it could have been a bomb that exploded when you shook it." He met Rarity's gaze. "Next time leave an unattended, unexpected box where it is and just call me."

"You're being a little dramatic, aren't you?" Rarity sat in one of the wing chairs.

When Drew didn't respond, but just kept staring, she held up her hands. "Fine, I won't pick up any unexpected packages without calling you first."

"Thank you." He went back and, using a pen, turned the shipping label forward to get a picture of Gay Zelda's name. "I don't think Gay mentioned that she was a patient of Dr. Conrad's as well."

"Would she?" Sam asked. "I mean, if you talked to me about someone killing an old friend, I'm not sure what doctors I was seeing would be part of the discussion."

"True." He used a rubber glove to pick up and sort through the bottles in the box. "Not the same ones as Martha, but definitely from the spa's brand."

"Everything is pointing to the spa," Rarity said.

"Except a motive. They want these people around to buy more of this crap." He put gloves on and picked up the box. "Let's get out of here. The bookstore is closing for the evening."

"Yes, sir." Rarity shot Drew a salute, which he ignored. She went and got her tote and Killer's bag. The little dog was at her heels the entire time. Archer took the bags.

"You grab Killer. You'll need a free hand to lock up."

Drew paused at the door. "The back door locked?"

"Yes, and the lights are out back there." Rarity pulled her keys out of her pocket and grabbed Killer, tucking him under one arm. "I've already checked, twice."

"Then let's get out of here." Drew paused at the door. "Thanks for calling me with this. I know I didn't say that before."

"You are welcome. And I didn't need a ride home." Rarity locked the door and turned to face the other three already out on the sidewalk.

"Tonight, you did." Archer nodded to a Jeep parked behind Drew's truck. "I'm over there."

When they arrived at Rarity's house, she was surprised when Archer got out too. She pulled out her keys. "I'm beat. I'd invite you in, but I don't think I'll be good company."

He took the keys from her. "Stay here, and I'll check out the house."

"You're kidding, right?" When he didn't answer, Rarity handed him her keys. "You don't have to go to the trouble."

"When I call Drew and let him know you're home, he'll ask if I checked the house. I don't lie." He smiled and tossed the keys in his hand. "It will only take a minute, and you don't want Drew dropping out of his mini date with Sam just to check on you, do you?"

"Go ahead, I surrender." Rarity laughed as he hurried to the front porch. He would call Drew and that would be exactly what Drew would do. Then Sam would blame her for the short date, and worse, accuse her of secretly liking Drew.

Killer whined as he licked her face.

"I know, you're tired and want to go to sleep. Just give Archer a few minutes, and then we can go inside." She glanced at her watch. It was almost ten. She looked over at Terrance's house, but it was dark. Her neighbor must be already asleep.

Early to bed, early to rise, just like her.

Archer came out and handed her back her keys. "All clear. I wanted to tell you the other night your backyard is amazing. I love that pool. I just have an apartment over the shop right now, but I'd kill to have a setup like this."

"Probably a bad choice of words since we're in the middle of a murder investigation." She started walking to the house, and Archer followed her with the two bags.

"True, but I don't think Martha's place has a swimming pool. At least not as nice as yours." He followed her just inside the house and set her bags on the floor. "Have a nice night."

"You need to get back to the island?" she asked.

"You know it." He paused at the door. "I'm taking a group back out to Devil's Bridge tomorrow morning at six if you want to come. No charge. I'd like your company."

"Sounds fun. If I don't oversleep, I'll be there." She watched as he jogged back to the Jeep. He waved as he backed it out of her driveway. Killer barked as he heard the car leave.

"Archer asked me to hike with him. Is that a date?" She shut the door and looked at the dog.

Killer didn't answer. Instead, he went to get a drink of water, leaving Rarity to figure out that answer all on her own.

* * * *

Rarity tossed and turned as she tried to sleep. She finally got up at five to get ready for her hike with Archer's group. She looked at the five different outfits she had laid out on the bed. In frustration, she grabbed a set of shorts and a tank that kind of matched and got dressed. "Not a date, a hike."

Killer barked his agreement.

"I'll come back and get you after the hike, and then we'll go into the store." She poured herself a travel mug of coffee and filled her backpack with a couple of granola bars and a bottle of water. She tucked her hair under her hat and put on the pack. "Watch the house, okay?"

Killer didn't respond; instead he went to lie back down in his bed. It was too early for him.

When she got to the hiking store, she saw Jonathon Anderson in the crowd. She waved, and he came over to meet her. "Good morning. Where's Edith?"

"She stayed in bed this morning. She's a little under the weather, so I thought I'd get out of her hair. We bought a book of hikes, so I've got unlimited hiking until the end of the season. I'm trying to make it worth the cost we paid. Archer's a good kid. We like to support him when we can." He nodded to her cup. "Good idea. I think I'll start bringing coffee to start my day. I only got one cup in before I left the house."

"Drew said he went to school with Archer. So you've known him a long time?" Rarity glanced around for the woman who was always answering the tour office phone when she called. "Do you know his wife?"

"Archer's not married." Jonathon frowned as he looked down at her. "Drew said he brought him over to your house on Sunday. He wouldn't do that if the guy was married. Drew has a strict moral code. He's always been that way. I think that's why he went into law enforcement. He thinks people should always do the right thing."

"Oh, I guess I thought that he worked with a spouse here at the tour office." Rarity could feel her cheeks heating up.

"No, that's Calliope. She's a college student and avid hiker. I think she wants Archer to hire her on as a guide when she graduates, but I'm not sure his business will be there in two years." He shrugged. "I probably shouldn't be telling you any of this, but I'm a freelance business consultant, so I've been helping Archer set up his business. He's a sharp kid, like I said before."

The bus pulled up and stopped in front of the shop. "There's our ride."

"After you." Jonathon held out his hand, and Rarity made her way to the bus line.

When she reached the top of the stairs, she met Archer's gaze. "I'm here."

"Glad you could make it. I'm sorry Killer isn't a little bigger so he could come along. I'd be afraid that something might happen to him on the trail as small as he is." Archer pulled her closer and waved Jonathon onto the bus. "I'm glad you made it, though."

"I was excited to be invited. Besides, Killer needs his beauty sleep. I'll go get him after this and take him to the bookstore." She grinned. "By the way, I'm going to have to order more trail books. The last ones you suggested are selling like hotcakes."

"That's what I like to hear. Go have a seat, and we'll get this party rolling." He turned to the next person in line. "Thanks for choosing Ender's Adventures. Do you have your ticket?"

As she made her way down the aisle, she saw Jonathon pointing at the seat in front of him. She slipped in next to an older woman. She tucked her backpack under her seat, then held out a hand. "Hi, I'm Rarity."

"Chloe Evans. I'm the pastor's wife, but don't hold that against me." The woman had bright silver hair cut in a pageboy and a smile that lit up the area around her. "Jonathon tells me you're the angel who took Killer in after Martha died. She loved that dog."

"I can see why. He's really special." Rarity settled in. "I take it you knew Martha well?"

"As well as she'd let anyone get to know her. Well, except Kelly. Man, she was head over heels over that guy. You couldn't tell her anything when it came to him." She glanced out the window. "He never was good enough for her."

"Now, dear, you don't know what goes on inside a relationship." A man sitting with Jonathon interrupted their conversation. "People have been trying to figure out why you stay with me for years."

"My husband, the joker." Chloe nodded toward him. "James, this is Rarity. She owns the bookstore downtown."

"Well, we will be good friends, then. I've been meaning to come in and order our books for next fall's Sunday school. We like to work with secular bookstores in our community to purchase our more widely available books. I'll send you an email. Do you have a card?" He leaned forward with his to offer her.

"Thanks, actually, I don't have one on me, but I'll shoot you an email as soon as I get back into the store today. I'd love to talk about how we can work together." Rarity looked up and saw Archer watching her in the rearview mirror. He smiled and gave her a thumbs-up. Had this been why he'd wanted her to come on the hike? To get her in touch with the Evanses and their book needs? She waved and turned back to Chloe. "Tell me more about Martha. I'd love to know more about her. Especially since I'm raising her dog."

Chloe told several stories about Martha, but by the time they got to the trailhead, Rarity hadn't learned anything new. Chloe was just finishing up a story about Martha's cancer journey when Pastor Evans interrupted her.

"Actually, she didn't have a second bout of cancer. Just before she died, she'd gone to a new doctor, and he'd said she was clear and had been clear for a while. She came to me, well, it must have been a few days before she died, and asked about forgiveness. I can't go into all that she said, since it's between a pastor and his charges, but she wasn't happy. I can tell you that."

"I'd heard that from someone else too," Rarity admitted and saw the look of relief on the pastor's face. "I can't believe someone would tell her something like that just to sell more product."

"Medicine isn't an exact science. Maybe her records got mixed up with someone else's? I told her to give the man the benefit of the doubt until after she'd talked to him. I hope it was all just a matter of miscommunication."

"Time to disembark," Archer called from the front. "Let's get our hike on before it gets too hot to handle out here."

"That's a great idea." Pastor Evans stood and motioned to Rarity to stand and move forward so Chloe could get out. "It was really nice meeting you, and if you're looking for a church family, come on by one Sunday. I swear you'll love it. We have an amazing choir, and the women's group is studying the application of Ruth in today's society."

"I'll think about it." She moved up the two steps that the person in front of her had made available so that she could let Chloe out.

"Now, James, don't scare the girl off. I like this one." Chloe smiled at Rarity and gently squeezed her shoulder. "We would love to have you attend. But I get it if you're too busy. Young people today are typically too busy for church until their lives change, and they start adding new members to their families."

"Well, I have Killer, and he's the only new member I intend to add to my family as far as I can tell. Thanks for letting me know a little more about Martha. I appreciate it. I'm taking Killer to the vet next week, and I'm not sure he's even the right one."

"Dr. Heinlein was Killer's vet. I'm sure they have all the records."

She blinked her eyes. Had it been that simple to get a real answer? "Thanks. That's not who I was scheduled to see. I'll get that changed up."

"Oh, anyone in his office would have access to his records."

"Actually, he's not even in the same office."

"Gay should have told you where to take Killer. She drove Martha there when Killer was sick. They thought they were going to lose him. Gay was such a good friend," Chloe said as they made their way off the bus.

"I didn't ask Madame—I mean, Gay—about the vet. I thought they weren't talking before Martha's death. That they were in a bad spot due to their husbands." Rarity tried to turn her head to watch the woman, but she couldn't see anyone behind her.

"Poppycock. That had been over for years. No one keeps a grudge going that long, not even over a man." Chloe glanced back, but the pastor was engaged in a conversation with Jonathon. "Martha wasn't happy with her life. And if she'd wanted something to happen, she'd have called Gay."

Rarity got ready for the hike, tucking her empty travel cup into her backpack. When she looked around, both Jonathon and the Evanses had left her behind. She was going to go talk to Madame Zelda again and see if there was anything else she'd left out.

Rarity blew a breath out and let her anger drain with it. A trick she'd learned from Sam and the yoga classes she was always trying to get Rarity to attend. It wasn't Madame Zelda's purpose on earth to make sure Rarity knew everything she needed to know. Maybe she'd thought Martha had left Killer with Rarity and that's how she'd come to have the small dog. But more than likely, she was just missing a friend.

Or she'd killed Martha and didn't want to talk about her for a whole different reason.

Chapter 18

Rarity paced on her deck as Sam checked the food on the grill again. "I swear, Sam, maybe I should just go over there and ask her point-blank if she knows who killed Martha."

"Great plan. Then when she shoots you and cuts your body up into little pieces, the only thing big enough to identify you will be a sample for a DNA test." Sam set the tongs down and went over to sit on the edge of the pool. "Come sit with me. You paid enough for this pool, you should use it more."

"I use it a lot. I swam Monday and Tuesday morning. The problem is, I'm not home a lot. Most nights I don't have time to swim or sit in the hot tub or even cook. Thanks for suggesting we grill outside tonight. I needed some girl time after today."

"So the hike didn't go well?" Sam patted the cement next to her.

Rarity pulled off her shoes and joined Sam on the stairs. "It was fun, but I think Archer knew the Evanses would be there and that's why he invited me. He wanted me to talk to them. So it wasn't a date. Or even a hike. It was a conversation starter. The problem is, I'm not sure I got the piece of information that he thought I might get once I talked to them. Other than the name of Killer's actual vet. Who knew there were two Yorkies in the area named Killer?"

"I could have probably guessed. I mean, it's a fun name for such a little dog," Sam said, but then quieted down when she saw the look from Rarity. "Anyway, so the preacher's wife didn't like Kelly, either. I'm with the others from the book club. I think this Kelly is our killer."

"But he has an alibi. At least according to Drew." She splashed her feet in the water. "Maybe you should talk to your boyfriend and have him double-check Kelly's alibi?"

"Whatever." Sam splashed water on Rarity.

"Rude." She grinned. "How long until dinner?"

"Probably twenty, thirty minutes. The potatoes are still hard." Sam stood. "Why?"

Rarity stood and headed into the house. "Because I'm doing my laps if we have that long. Do you still have a suit here in the guest room?"

"Of course." Sam followed her into the house. "But don't blame me if dinner gets overdone."

"I'll check it halfway into my laps. I just need to burn off some of this energy. I can't believe we still don't know who killed Martha. According to all those books, finding a killer is really easy. And they even have time to develop recipes to put in the back." Rarity hurried into her room to change. It was time for some Rarity time to clear her head. She'd worry about Martha's death tomorrow.

After her swim, they enjoyed dinner—and they talked about anything but Martha.

The next morning, Rarity taped a sign to the front window saying she'd be opening the store at 1 p.m. and then locked the door. She had Killer and his dog bag in one arm. It was time to visit the vet to set up his file. She gave the little dog a kiss on his head. "It's like it's adoption day. Once we switch over your medical records, you'll officially be my puppy."

Killer gave a quick yip that might have meant, *Wow, that's cool.* At least that's what Rarity wanted the yip to mean. She set him into the Jeep on the passenger side and put his dog bag on the floor. Then she went around to the driver's side to get in. Pulling out onto the street, she thought she saw Madame Zelda watching her from her studio window, but when she glanced back, the window was empty.

"Nope, no one is going to burst my bubble today. No talk of murder on adoption day, right, Killer?" She glanced over and saw he'd curled up into a circle and was going to sleep. "I can see you're overwrought with excitement. I'll just turn on some music and you can relax a little until we get to Flagstaff."

A little ways out of town, her phone rang. She punched a button on her steering wheel. "This is Rarity."

"Good, since that's who I called. Where are you going this morning? Don't you have to open the bookstore?" Archer asked.

"I left a note. I'm taking Killer to the vet to change over his paperwork to my name. I'll tell you, he's over the moon about it being adoption day." She glanced at the sleeping Killer.

"Killer? He's excited?"

She laughed, hearing the disbelief. "Well, he will be as soon as he wakes up from his nap. So, why are you checking on me? How did you know I wasn't in town?"

"You passed by where I store the bus a few minutes ago. I've got a group I'm taking out in a few minutes. I was going to ask if you wanted to come with us since I kind of set you up the last time."

"I knew it. You wanted me to talk to the Evanses and find out more about Martha." She tapped her fingers on the steering wheel. "You're going to get in trouble with Drew."

"Not if you don't rat me out. Sam told me your book group is playing Sherlock Holmes, so I thought you might like a chance to chat with Chloe. There's not anything that goes on around town that deals with her husband's flock that she doesn't know. Did you get some good info?"

She thought about her talk with Chloe. "I'm not sure. She didn't like Kelly O'Reilly at all. But Drew says he's got an alibi."

"Just because you say you were somewhere doesn't mean you were. I know Drew's a thorough guy, but what if O'Reilly just is a good storyteller?"

"That could be true, but it feels off."

He laughed, and the sound echoed in the Mini. Killer looked up from his bed and then laid his head back down when he realized it was coming from the speakers. "I'd tell you to go talk to our local fortune teller, but she's on the suspect list too. Anyway, I've got to get this group going. I'll call you another time."

"Sounds good." She ended the connection and focused on the road ahead. "So, Archer wants to be part of the sleuthing group, huh?"

Killer didn't respond, but then she heard a small snore coming from her passenger. At least she had something to think about while she drove. Well, two things. What was Archer's motivation? And of course, who had killed Martha.

By the time she got to Flagstaff, she had a headache. It was probably from the heat, but she blamed her rambling about Martha for the pain. She parked at the vet's office and pointed to the drive-in just up the street. "When we get done, we're going to grab a hamburger, fries, and a shake for the drive home. What? Don't look at me that way, I know it's only ten o'clock."

She scooped up Killer and her tote. She had a few questions for the vet staff that she wanted to get answers to, including his birthday and any health issues he'd had or might have due to the breed.

She filled out the new patient information, then asked if she could talk to someone about Killer's history. It took a few minutes for the vet tech to get free to talk to her, but when she came out, Killer wiggled in Rarity's arms. She took the clipboard from Rarity and glanced over the information that Rarity had filled in.

"Hi, I'm Janie. Killer and I are friends. What can I help you with, Rarity?" Janie sat next to her, Killer's original file on her lap.

"I was wondering if you could tell me about Killer's medical history. What's his birthday? Did he have any issues as a pup? Anything special I should be feeding him or watching out for?" She opened her notebook and held the pen to the paper, waiting for answers.

"Actually, I'm so happy you're taking this adoption seriously. So many people just see how cute a dog is and don't realize they might have issues." Janie scanned the file. "His birthday is April eighth. He was two this year. Martha got him from Yorkie Love Kennels in Phoenix, so we have his original shot records and vet notes from there. I'll transfer that over to your file with a summary of his health record. We'll keep Martha's file, too, and reference that in case something goes wrong and we need to look back."

Rarity rubbed Killer on the back, and he lay down between the two women, content.

"But no, he didn't have much going on, just normal visits. She bought her flea and tick products from us, so I can get that set up for you today. I'm sure he hasn't had a treatment for a while, but I would wait thirty days from when you got him to apply more. Just in case. He's so little."

Walking out of the vet office, Rarity was a little under two hundred dollars lighter with all the meds and food they suggested. She'd probably keep him on the higher-end food that she'd been feeding him, but at least she knew he'd been well cared for during his time with Martha.

"Okay, so you don't need your shots until next April again." She tucked him into the car and glanced up at the drive-in. Now it was almost eleven, and she could eat while she drove. That would save some time. She might have the store open before one, depending on how slow the drive-in line went.

Her phone rang when she was halfway to Sedona. She set the milkshake down and answered the call. "This is Rarity."

"Hi, Rarity, it's Janie. I found a new note for Killer's file and thought you might want to know. He was brought in a few weeks ago with an injured leg. The man who brought him in said he'd jumped off the bed and had been limping. The notes weren't in his file because the man paid in cash and we didn't connect the dog with Martha. I guess the guy called him something else when he came in. Anyway, they took X-rays and nothing was broken, but if he favors his left leg or seems to be in pain, bring him back in for more tests."

"Thanks for letting me know. Hey, did you get the man's name?" It had to be Kelly. What, had he attacked Martha's dog? Or maybe tried to break into her house and Killer had gotten in the way?

"No, no name. And like I said, he paid cash. Our new vet, Annie, saw you go out and pulled the record since we'd been trying to find who the incident should be filed with."

"Thanks for calling. I'll watch him." She disconnected, and after a second, called Drew. When he picked up, he didn't sound like he was in a good mood.

"Look, I've been busy this week. I don't have time for coffee."

"Nice to know, but that's not why I'm calling."

Drew swore. "Sorry, I thought it was my mom calling. She's been harping on me to take Sam out all week."

"Didn't you tell her you cooked her dinner on Sunday?"

He sighed. "I wish I'd thought of that. Anyway, what can I do for you?"

"Did Martha report a break-in at her house a couple of weeks before she died?" Rarity paused and took a sip of her milkshake while she waited for the answer.

"That is oddly specific. And, as it happens, true. Martha was called out of town unexpectedly and thought she'd be home earlier than she was. When she got home late that night, a window in the back door had been broken in, but she didn't report that anything was taken. How on earth did you know?"

"Funny thing, a man took Killer to the vet right about the same time and told them the dog had fallen off the bed. He paid for the visit in cash."

"You think someone broke into Martha's house and hurt Killer? Then took him to the vet? All before Martha got home?"

"Yeah, I'm beginning to think that exact thing." She paused, then added the other thing she'd wanted to say. "I think it was Kelly. I bet if you take his picture down to the vet clinic, someone might recognize him."

When she got to the store, her mail was tucked into her box. She pulled it out, unlocked the door, and let Killer down into the cool air. He ran straight to the water dish, then went back to the door and sat. He didn't look like he was limping or favoring his leg at all.

"You need outside, huh?" She tucked her purse under the counter and took the mail out to the front, where she had a piece of green outdoor carpet on the side of the walkway for Killer's use. She had a second one in the back, for when the front was in full sunlight. She flipped through the envelopes as she waited for him to find the perfect spot.

Bill, junk, bill, junk, and a postcard from the hospital in St. Louis. Her mammogram was due. She needed to get in touch with a new doctor, but she could call and get the test scheduled now. She checked on Killer, who was now sitting quietly at the end of his leash, watching and waiting for her.

"Let's get the day going."

He followed her into the store, and after being taken off his lead, ran to his bed. Apparently sleeping in the car on the way there and back hadn't been enough of a nap for him. It was round two. She went to the counter and made a call to the local hospital. It took a few transfers, but finally, she was talking with someone who not only made her an appointment for the test, but also a check-in with a nurse practitioner. She could refer her to another doctor if they decided Rarity needed more oversight.

She keyed the appointments into her phone, then opened her planner and did the same. She turned back to her monthly goals and scratched off one. Then she threw away the postcard. "Done and done."

The door opened, and Archer came inside. "You found your way back."

"Pretty easy. Just one highway between the two towns. What are you doing?" She watched as he came up to the counter.

"I wanted to give you another book to add to your collection. I'm adding it to my list of suggestions, so hopefully it will get you some more sales." He handed her a sheet of paper. As she keyed in the information, he looked around the store. "I'm sure business will pick up soon."

She nodded. "Between your hikers and Shirley's husband's love of World War II, I've been doing okay with sales."

"Shirley?" He looked at her, frowning.

"One of my book club members. She's a hoot." She nodded as the computer displayed the information about the book. "We're in luck. It's still in print, so I'll have some in stock next week. I've also reordered all the ones you gave me the last time we talked, so I have to say, I appreciate the help."

"No problem." He tapped his fingers on the counter, then started to say something.

Rarity watched as he shook his head. Apparently, he'd changed his mind.

"Anyway, I'll give you a call when I have another hike scheduled. Maybe next week?"

She nodded, thinking that wasn't what he had been going to say, but she left it alone. "Maybe next week."

She watched him walk out the door and pause at the sidewalk. Something was bothering Archer. Maybe he'd tell her the next time they talked, or maybe she'd just missed the chance.

Chapter 19

Sam showed up with coffee on Friday morning when Rarity arrived at the bookstore. She set the coffee and a bag on the counter. "Good morning."

Rarity looked inside the bag. "There's only one donut."

"I thought you'd be in earlier, and I was hungry. I bought four. I'm stuffed." She pulled a stool around the counter and sat. "Anyway, I have an outing for us. Edith called last night and asked if we were coming, so technically we've been invited."

"Invited to what?" She took the donut out and took a bite. Pure sugar heaven.

"Martha's funeral. They're having it today at three at the church. I think we should close the stores and head down there. The other book club members agree, and they're going to meet us there." She downed what was left of her coffee. She held up the cup. "Did you make any yet?"

"You followed me in. I haven't even turned on all the lights yet." She used her thumb to point toward the break room. "You know where everything is. Let me get set up, and we can talk about this idea of yours."

"This *great* idea of mine," Sam restated. She moved around the counter and disappeared into the back.

Killer was standing by the fireplace watching. He whined quietly.

"I know. Your godmother is a little heavily caffeinated. Or it might be the sugar. If I were you, I'd pretend I was asleep on my bed until she leaves." Rarity smiled as Killer followed her instructions and ran to the bed near the fireplace.

"I heard that," Sam called from the back.

Chuckling, Rarity went through her opening checklist. When she'd first bought the store, she'd just wandered through the day. Then she read a book about efficiency that had introduced her to opening and closing rituals and checklists. It had made all the difference—especially on the last working day of the week and the first one.

By the time she'd finished, Sam was back with a glass of orange juice and the last of the cookies from Tuesday's book club. "So, anyway, I was talking to Edith, and she thought we should come to the funeral. Especially since you took on Killer. Maybe we'll learn something about Martha that we didn't know. Or see someone looking suspicious."

"Maybe they'll wear a sign that says, *I killed Martha*. That way we'll know who to talk to." Rarity sipped her coffee.

"Don't be silly. Like I said, I talked to everyone in the club but Kim. She's never home when I call her. Don't get me wrong, she always calls back, but I can never get her to answer on first contact." Sam pursed her lips as she thought about a reason someone wouldn't want to attend a funeral. "And Drew can't complain, since it was his mom who invited us."

"Oh, I think he'll still complain. It's just he'll get the backlash from his mom when he does." Rarity thought about the advantages for going to the funeral. "I guess we could finally meet the mystery man Martha was dating. I'd like to think I'm a good judge of character, but frankly, his misdeeds while they were dating makes me not like him now."

"Great, I'll see you at two, then. We'll need to run home and change into something black. Then I'll meet you outside the church. Don't go in without me. I'll tell the rest of the group to meet us outside, that way we can show a united front. She *was* part of our book club." Forgetting about the coffee she'd made, Sam hurried to the doorway.

"She was only at one meeting," Rarity reminded her.

"She was still a book club member. And we want to be seen as caring people." Sam hurried out of the shop as some real shoppers came inside.

"Good morning," Rarity called out to the newcomers, hoping they hadn't heard Sam's last words, but they probably had. Especially from the shocked look on the woman's face. "Anything I can help you with?"

"Archer sent us over to check out the hiking trail books?" The man hurried toward the counter, ignoring his wife's hesitancy.

"Oh yes, I just restocked that entire section. Everyone wants to be as knowledgeable about the area as Archer."

The woman relaxed and followed after her husband.

The rest of the day was busy, but not too busy for Rarity to think closing early was a bad idea. She had several people who were looking for books to get them through their week in Sedona. Some were spouses who didn't love the hiking, but who put up a good show for the good of their marriage. They bought self-help books, cookbooks, romances, and women's fiction.

When two o'clock came around, she'd been alone in the store for over thirty minutes. She put up the sign she'd made saying she'd reopen in the morning. She got Killer and his stuff and her own treasures ready and locked up the store. She headed home to drop off Killer and change her clothes.

Arriving at the church, sans Killer in tow, she found Shirley first. The older woman threw her arms around Rarity and gave her a quick hug. "I'm so glad you came. I wondered after Sam was so insistent on this outing. I'm not entirely convinced we'll be welcome, but you never know if you don't try."

The crowd seemed welcoming if a bit sparce. Rarity watched people walk inside the church. "The woman lived here all her life, and no one can be bothered with coming to her funeral?"

"For Sedona, this *is* a good turnout. It's too hot at three to do graveside services, so it will all be held here at the church. Speaking of the heat, we might want to wait inside for the others." Shirley fanned herself with a program she'd already gotten from inside the church lobby.

Rarity realized Shirley must have been waiting inside and just came out to see if anyone was here. "Sorry, I didn't think about the heat. I've got my phone on, so when the others get here, I'll round them up."

"Sounds perfect." Shirley moved toward the doorway, and Rarity followed her.

"I'm surprised your husband didn't come as well. I'd love to meet him." Rarity had reached over to open the door so she saw Shirley's lips tighten. *Uh-oh*, she thought. *They must have gotten into a squabble about attending.*

"He's busy with one of his models. I guess it's giving him problems." Shirley stepped into the foyer. "Besides, he hates things like this. I swear, he won't even come to his own funeral unless we lock him into the casket."

Rarity chuckled and was going to ask another question when she saw Holly, Malia, and Sam standing near the watercooler. "There's the gang. I guess they all had the same idea."

They moved through the few people still in the foyer and met up with the rest of the club members. Sam pulled a piece of white string off Rarity's black suit. "Sorry, it was just too hot to wait outside, especially dressed in black. I swear, they should have made the rule that you had to wear white to funerals. Less people would get sick from heatstroke."

Malia giggled. "Technically, you don't have to wear black, just something respectful. I have this black-patterned dress that I keep for any funerals I have to attend. Which, thankfully, isn't many. It makes my skin crawl a little being at one, especially after the cancer scare."

"I feel the same way. I just keep thinking, *What if?*" Holly shook the idea off like it was water on a duck's back. "Anyway, we're here for Martha, not us."

"Did you just see Kim walk into the chapel?" Shirley tapped Rarity's arm. "I called and left her a message but didn't hear back. Maybe she thinks we're inside?"

"Well, we'd better get inside if we don't want to be late." Sam glanced at her watch. "Hopefully there are still five chairs for us."

"Pews. And yes, with this crowd, I think we'll be fine." Shirley adjusted her suit and moved toward the door.

When they got inside, they saw Pastor Evans and the choir entering the sanctuary. Apparently, they were just in time. They slipped into a pew about halfway back that had enough room for all of them.

Rarity scanned the other pews. She didn't see Kim at all. She leaned toward Shirley. "What was Kim wearing?"

"A black dress," Shirley whispered back.

Great. That really narrowed the crowd. She sat and went through all the pews on her side without finding the missing club member.

And before she could check out the other side, Pastor Evans started talking. She leaned back and paid attention, a skill her grandmother had tried to teach her every Sunday from as far back as she could remember. Her parents hadn't attended church, but Grandma Hettie hadn't missed a Sunday. At least not before she'd been admitted to a local long-term care facility. She hadn't lived long after that, and this funeral reminded Rarity of her grandmother's service.

When they'd finished, they moved into the great room for punch, coffee, and cookies. A mini wake for Martha. The book club gathered together as Rarity held a Styrofoam cup in one hand and a napkin with a few cookies in her other hand.

"Well, wasn't that lovely?" Chloe Evans asked as she came by and greeted the women.

Rarity nodded. "It was just the right bit of humor mixed with sadness. I'm glad your husband brought up Killer."

"Believe me, he was going to call out for someone to take the dog home with them if he hadn't found out that you'd already stepped up. Thanks for doing that."

"No problem. I love the little guy." Rarity looked past Chloe and saw Kim hurrying toward the door. "Hold on a second. I just saw someone I know."

"That tends to happen at funerals. I'll let you all chat. I know you need to catch up with people you haven't seen." Chloe moved to the next small group.

"Kim? Is that you?" Rarity didn't want to yell, but she couldn't just hurry after her either. The crowd might be small, but they were packed in the small social area.

Kim heard her somehow, and when she caught Rarity's gaze, she held up a finger. Then Rarity watched as she leaned over to a man who looked a lot like Dr. Conrad. If she was to be honest with herself, it looked exactly like Dr. Conrad. What on earth was Kim doing with him?

"Guys, I can't believe you're here." Kim hurried over on stiletto heels that matched the little black dress that was more suited for a cocktail party than a funeral. "I'm so sorry I haven't been able to get to the meetings lately, work has been crazy."

"I guess, with your medical appointments, it's made it worse." Shirley patted Kim on the back. "You know they have to let you off for medical treatments. It's not like in the past, when they could just fire you."

"You say that like it's true." Kim shook her head. "I don't want anyone knowing about the…thing. I can't stand to see the pity in their eyes."

Everyone around the group but Sam nodded.

"It's hard when everyone thinks you're going to die," Malia said, and Holly squeezed her hand.

"That's why we have the group. We're more likely to tease you than give you pity." Rarity glanced at the man who was now leaving the church. "I'm sorry, was that Dr. Conrad?"

A second passed, and Rarity thought Kim wasn't going to answer. Finally, she nodded. "Yes, that's my boss. I'm his personal assistant, so I'm responsible for all his appearances and a lot of other things. Like this funeral. Martha was one of his clients. He thought the world of her."

Rarity bit her tongue. She wanted to ask if Kim knew that the good doctor sold supplements to his clients whether or not they needed them or really had cancer. But Kim only handled his personal calendar, so maybe she didn't know. Then an idea hit her. "He's not your personal oncologist, is he?"

Kim's eyes widened, and she shook her head quickly. "Oh no. I don't want him to know. He might insist that I take off time, and then where would I be? Alone in my apartment? No way."

"You're right." Shirley took her arm. "Staying busy is much better. Do you have time for some coffee and pie?"

Kim dropped her gaze. "I'd love to, but I have to get back to work. Dr. Conrad is holding the car for me, as we've got to get his travel plans set for the next convention."

"We won't hold you up, then. It was just so nice seeing you." Shirley gave Kim a big hug, and the rest of the group waved as she headed out the door.

"Well, that's a twist in the story. Thank goodness she's not taking the supplements like Martha was." Holly glanced around the group. "Are we still on for coffee and pie? This coffee is awful and the cookies are stale."

They found a table at Annie's Bakery, and after getting their order in, they sat around the table and talked about who they'd seen at the funeral.

Holly sipped her coffee. "I don't know most of those people, but shouldn't Madame Zelda have been there?"

"She was." Shirley wiped the table with a few napkins before setting her purse on her lap. "She was up front with Kelly O'Reilly. He had the shock of red hair? Gay wasn't in her psychic costume, just a classic black dress."

"Kim's dress was more *va-va-voom* than secretarial." Malia looked around the table. "Don't tell me everyone else wasn't thinking it."

"Thinking it and saying it are two different things," Shirley pointed out. "Anyway, Kim is one of us, not one of our suspects."

The waitress brought over the pie, and conversation stopped for a few minutes. Finally, when everyone was done eating, Rarity looked around the table. "Okay, so we know where two of the suspects were at the funeral. Any idea where anyone else was located?"

"Drew's dad and mom were on the same side as we were," Holly offered.

Rarity frowned. "I didn't think Jonathon was still on the suspect list."

"He is until we find out who did kill Martha," Malia said, glancing at her watch. "I've got a shift over at the Garnet in an hour. I better go get changed."

"I'll walk out with you." Holly stood and pushed her chair in. "I know you like the guy, but we don't have a lot of suspects here."

"Maybe that's our problem. We need more suspects. Did you find out anything more about Martha's will or the house?"

"Interestingly enough, I did." She grinned at Malia, who was waiting for her. "And to find out, you're going to have to be at our next book club meeting."

The two women left, and Sam focused on her coffee. "Both of them are great with foreshadowing suspense."

"It's their age." Shirley stood. "I need to get going as well. George likes to eat early. We're old like that."

Rarity laughed and waved at Shirley. "Have a good night, but don't expect me to think of you or your husband as old. You're both so active."

Shirley fluffed her hair. "If I just keep running, no one, including death, will ever be able to catch me."

As she walked out the door, Rarity looked at Sam. "So, a waste of time?"

"I'm not sure. I think there's more to the story than we're able to see. I really wish we knew who was Martha's heir. Then we could turn the oversized spotlight on him." Sam took the last bite of her pie. "At least we got some good pie out of the deal."

Chapter 20

Saturday at the bookstore was super busy. Rarity was writing down books to order as fast as they were selling. If she had the updated software, it would have kept her shopping list for her. Instead, she had to manually enter the books she wanted to replace. A number of people stopped in and picked up the trail books that Archer had encouraged as supplemental reading for his tours. She was going to have to take him to dinner for his push. Maybe she could partner with other businesses in town to see what kinds of books their patrons would like.

It was an idea. She wrote it down in her notebook where she kept all her bright and shiny ideas. When she had time, she'd do more research, but this was a great place to store it until she was ready to dig in. She ordered takeout from the Garnet for lunch and was surprised when Malia walked through the door with her order. "Lunch is served."

"I was planning on shutting down and going to get it. You didn't have to bring it over."

Malia shrugged. "I wasn't doing anything anyway. And that creep was in the bar. He can be pretty handsy, so I just stay out of there when he starts drinking."

"Do I know this creep?" Rarity wanted to give the guy a kick in the nether regions if she did.

"Kind of. You know of him. It's Kelly O'Reilly. He thinks everyone wants him, when really, he's my grandfather's age. Like ever." Malia mimed sticking her finger down her throat and throwing up.

"Okay, I didn't like him before, and this just moves the needle further toward the creep category. I wish we had some solid evidence to give Drew that he killed Martha. It would kill two birds with one stone." A thought started to form as Rarity unpacked her lunch. She looked at Malia. "Do you know if his realty office is open on Mondays?"

She shrugged. "I think so. He typically hangs out at the Garnet on weekends, so I guess he works the other times."

"I think I'm going to call and make an appointment for Monday morning and see if I can find out where he was when Martha died. If we can break his alibi, Drew will have to look at him again." She unwrapped the French dip. "I love this sandwich. It's the best one I've had from there."

"I love the avocado toast they serve at lunch." Malia's phone beeped. She glanced at the display. "And I have another delivery. If I'm lucky, I may be out of the building for the rest of the day."

After Malia left, Rarity looked up the realty phone number and made the call. "Hi, this is Rarity Cole, owner of The Next Chapter. The local bookstore? I'd like to talk to you about a marketing idea that might be good for both of our businesses. Will you be available at nine on this coming Monday? I'll stop by then, but give me a call if you won't be at the shop."

She left her cell number and hung up. She ate her lunch and then took Killer outside for a bit. When she came back inside, she wandered through the bookshelves, restocking books that had been left out and making notes of any of the bestsellers that were close to being out of copies.

Then she went back to the counter and waited on customers to come into the shop. After an hour had passed without the door opening, she glanced over at Killer. "What do you think? Close up early? Maybe switch out our open times to mornings and evenings?"

She wondered if her accounting system would tell her when the most sales happened. She opened her computer and started looking at reports that she could run. As she did this, the bell over the door rang. She glanced up, thinking her busyness could have brought in someone. She waved at the newcomer. "Kim, come on in. It nice to see you."

"Better than our last meeting, right?" Kim shut the door and hurried over to the counter, pausing to snatch a thriller that Rarity had just gotten in that week. "I don't have a lot of time, but I needed a new book. I also wanted to follow up on our conversation about you looking for a local oncologist. Have you found someone?"

"Not yet. I scheduled a mammogram, and the office there set me up to meet someone afterward to at least review my chart. They said if I didn't like this one, they had more choices available." Rarity scanned the book. "Why?"

Kim pulled out a credit card, then replaced it and pulled out another one. *Kim Hunt* was printed on the card. "I just wanted to put a plug in for the practice where I work. Dr. Conrad is amazing and has a really high survival rate for his patients. That's what you really want in a doctor who deals with cancer, am I right?"

Rarity wrote Kim's name in her notebook. She hadn't written down Kim's last name when she came to the book club. And it was hard to add people to a mailing list without a name or email address. "I don't know. I visited the spa where Dr. Conrad works, and it just felt a little off. So you work there too?"

"I don't work at the spa, I work in the main offices in Flagstaff. Like I said, I'm more about scheduling his appearances and such." She took back her credit card. "Seriously, Rarity, I'm worried about you. I want to make sure you have the best care. You should at least schedule a visit. I can set it up for you."

Rarity tucked the receipt into the book and handed it back to Kim. "Sorry, I'm just not into all of the New Age stuff. I want a doctor who is affiliated with one of the local cancer facilities. They have the history and experience dealing with these things."

"But, Rarity," Kim started, but Rarity held up a hand.

"No. I'm not going there. Martha went there. I know the spa didn't kill her, but it sounded like it gave her false hope. I'm all about being positive during treatment and staying upbeat. But that place is way too woo-woo for me. Malia would probably like it. Maybe it's my age, but I want a real doctor."

"Dr. Conrad *is* a *real* doctor." Kim spun around on her heel and hurried out of the bookstore. She slammed the door after her.

Killer stood and barked at the door as the sound woke him from his nap.

Rarity went over and picked him up, hugging him close. "It's okay, buddy. Kim just didn't like what I was saying about her boss. I guess I need to learn to keep my opinions a little closer to my chest."

Killer licked her on the hand, and Rarity set him back down. She checked the time. Almost five. She'd been open long enough for a Saturday. At least until she figured out how to use the purchase reporting download she'd just found. But that was a project for Tuesday. She had already set up her hours for Tuesday through Saturday for the rest of the month. She'd look at the facts before making any more changes.

She decided to lock up. It was time for the weekend and maybe even a glass of wine after the run-in she'd just had with Kim.

Sam called on her phone right after she and Killer arrived home. "Where are you?"

"I shut down early, why?" Rarity set Killer's food down on the floor and picked up his water dish to rinse and refill it.

"I was going to see if you wanted to eat dinner with me at the Garnet."

Rarity set the water dish down and took the phone out to the deck. "Sorry, I ate lunch there. I'm just going to grill something here and have a salad. You can come over if you want."

"No, I already told Holly I'd meet her there. I just didn't want you to be alone. Everything okay?"

"Everything's fine. I'll tell you about my day another time. Go have fun. Tell Holly I said hi." She ended the conversation and then looked at Killer, who'd finished eating and was out on the deck watching her. "Sam's having dinner with Holly, and I saw Malia earlier today. We're beginning to fit into Sedona. I have friends besides just Sam now."

Killer lay down, still watching her.

"Yeah, I know, I probably lost a potential friend in Kim today. But some people just aren't meant to fit into our social circle." She stood up. "I'm swimming before dinner, then I think we should find a movie to watch and have some popcorn. It's date night."

Killer's ears perked up at the word *popcorn*. Rarity had found the little dog had an affinity for the microwaved treat a few weeks ago when she'd first gotten him.

He made her smile. And right now, that was all the social interaction she wanted.

* * * *

The next morning, Sam showed up at the house with muffins. Rarity opened the door, then picked up the almost-empty bag of popcorn off the end table to throw away.

"Wild night at home?" Sam asked as she set the muffins on the counter.

"Movie and popcorn. I'm surprised Killer didn't sneak out of the bedroom last night and finish it off." Rarity poured another cup of coffee and set it in front of Sam. She grabbed napkins and opened the plastic case around the muffins. "How was dinner with Holly?"

"Both Holly and Malia showed up. Malia was just getting off her shift so she joined us. I guess she talked to you earlier yesterday?" Sam took a muffin and set it on a napkin, breaking a bite off.

"She delivered my lunch. She says that this Kelly guy is a real piece of work." Rarity sipped her coffee and watched Killer out on the deck chasing bugs.

"Malia said you're going to go talk to him at his realty office. Do you think that's a good idea?" Sam pointed a new piece of muffin at her before popping it into her mouth. "What if he really killed Martha? Do you want to be alone with him?"

"Good point. You can come with me. On another subject I need you to come up with three or four books for me to order for your customers. Maybe something like the power of crystals in healing? Not too out there, but something tourists would buy to take home and learn more about your shop." Rarity had made a list last night during the movie of possible shops she could do a book venture with. "I'll pay for the bookmarks—they will have the names of your shop, my store, and the three or four books you recommend."

"'Available at The Next Chapter'? I like it. Great idea."

"Thanks, but I can't take credit for it. It was Archer who came up with it. And he did all the marketing for it. I should thank him. Maybe invite him to dinner or something." Rarity pulled out her planner. "Or I could take him cookies?"

"I think you should invite him to dinner. That way, you can figure out if he's interested in you or just the potential marketing adventure." Sam sipped her coffee. "Are you going into town for groceries today?"

"I thought I would sometime this weekend. Do you want to tag along?"

Sam nodded. "Can I? I am totally out of food since I was working on stock all last weekend for the convention. And today would be better. Unless you have plans."

"No plans either today or tomorrow. Do you have your list with you? Or do you want to go this afternoon?"

"I have my list. I'm a good scout. I'm always prepared. Although I don't think that was the Girl Scout motto. Anyway, I can leave anytime you're ready."

"Let me finish my coffee. I want to ask you something." Rarity went through her conversation with Kim the day before. When she finished, she didn't meet Sam's gaze. "Do you think I was insensitive?"

"You're kidding, right?" Sam refilled her cup. "If I remember the first conversation about this, she was pushy then, too, about her 'doctor.' Maybe she gets a bonus for bringing people in? You know, like a referral fee?"

"I hadn't thought of that. It felt more personal than just money, though." Rarity thought about the support groups she'd gone to in St. Louis. "I remember one lady got kicked out of one of my support groups the year I was in treatment because she was pushing her own line of skin care treatment. Radiation is really damaging to the skin, so having a good skin cream is crucial. I guess she was selling it out of her trunk after the meetings. I never got asked, but one of the ladies told me later it was amazing."

"I guess you lucked out, then." Sam nodded to the sink. "The stuff you have over there is really nice. I tried to buy it on my last shopping trip, and it was way out of my price range. So I sneak some when I come over here."

"No wonder you're always so willing to do the dishes." Rarity made a mental note about buying Sam some bottles of the cream for her birthday. "It is pricey, but I agree it's magic on dry skin."

"I didn't like the higher-priced stuff at the spa, though. It was all too flowery-scented, and the lotion was a little watered down, didn't you think?" Sam walked over to the sink and squirted some of the cocoa butter hand cream on her hands. "The smell of this makes me think I'm on the beach relaxing. The stuff at the spa smelled like the church with all those funeral flowers."

"You're so bad." Rarity finished her coffee and went to let Killer inside. "I just need to change clothes. I'll be ready in five minutes."

"I'll chat with my favorite little man, then." Sam clapped her hands and called Killer forward. "What are you dragging around? Is this one of your babies?"

"He loves his toys." Rarity moved toward the bedroom.

"Rarity, I don't think this is one of his toys. I think it was meant for you." Sam held up a baby doll that had had her eyes punched out and a noose around her neck. The rope was what Killer had used to drag the doll inside. It was almost as big as he was. He jumped to try to take the doll away from Sam, thinking this was another game. But it wasn't a game. At least not one that either Killer or Rarity should be playing. "There's a note. 'Stop sticking your nose where it doesn't belong. Or else.'"

Rarity pointed to the table. "Set it there. And call Drew. We need him over here."

By the time Drew got there and had his officers canvassing the neighborhood, the morning was gone. Rarity leaned back in her chair, her arms behind her head. "I hate to tell you to leave, but how much longer are you going to be here?"

He looked up from his notebook. "Why? Do you have a date?"

"Yes." When his head jerked up, she laughed. "Sam and I were planning to go to the grocery store this morning. Now it's almost noon, and with this heat, my ice cream is going to melt before we get it home."

"Take a cooler with those ice pack things. That's what Mom does."
He looked up from his notes. "I can lock up if you want to go. I just want
everyone to finish their canvassing before I go back to the station."

"I hope someone got pictures of whoever did this. I'm getting a little
tired of not knowing my enemy." She rubbed her neck.

He started to say something, then paused as his phone rang. "Sorry,
got to get this." He answered with one word, then nodded and grunted
through the conversation. When he finished, he wrote a few things down,
then stood up, closing his leather notebook. "I'll be out of your hair, then.
If you have to go into Flagstaff today, just be careful."

"The canvassing is done. Did anyone see anything?" Rarity tried to
watch Drew's expression. The man had a horrible poker face. She could
have guessed the answer before he spoke.

"No. Everyone has been out or not answering when the officer knocked.
We'll reach out to those home owners, but a lot of these houses are vacation
homes. When it's hot, like it is this week, they stay home." This time he
looked her straight in the eye. "And we don't know when it was thrown in
your yard. Terrance says you have a lot of people over."

"You, Archer, and Sam are considered a freaking crowd to Terrance.
Oh, and when you break into my back yard," Rarity nodded to the doll in
a bag on the table, "Don't forget your evidence. I'd throw it away if I had
to look at it much longer."

"Rarity, I'm trying. It's just that there's the murder, and now this?
Maybe I made a mistake sending you to the spa. Maybe that's what has
you in the killer's line of sight."

"What?" Rarity said. But it came out more like a high-pitched squeak
and not a real word. "You think it's someone from the spa?"

He picked up the doll and stared at it through the bag. "I didn't say
that. But do me a favor. Stay away from that place. I don't want either of
you or any of your freaking book club members to come even steps away
from the spa. I would hate to scare someone into doing something stupid."

Chapter 21

On Monday morning, a knock sounded at her front door. With Killer at her feet, Rarity went and opened it. She'd been up and at the table for a few hours already, working on a plan for the rest of the year. She needed to find some hobbies that were a little less intense. Like maybe skydiving. "Terrance. What are you doing up this early? I thought I was the only one with a built-in alarm clock. Do you want to come in for coffee?"

"No, that's fine. I just wanted to check on you to see if you were okay. I saw the cops were here a long time on Saturday." His brown eyes gleamed with the hint of gossip.

"Not much to say. Just a lot of paperwork. I wish it was more exciting, like in the movies, but I guess that's just acting, right?" She leaned against the doorjamb like she didn't feel she could stand unassisted much longer.

"Oh, I'm sorry to have bothered you. I know it can be stressful. Just know I'll be watching your house from now on. Just in case. I would hate to have anything happen to my favorite neighbor."

"From what the police said, we might be the only ones here through the heat wave." She waved toward the empty houses. "I don't get spending so much money for a house and just letting it sit unoccupied. If this was my vacation house, I would be coming here every weekend if it was up to me."

"They're mostly older people. They live in one house until they're bored, then move to the next. I like staying put, myself. It helps me pretend I have roots." He smiled gently, but Rarity could see the emotion didn't hit his eyes.

"You have roots. You've been the only neighbor who has even reached out. So you have me." She glanced down at Killer. "Are you part of any civic or community groups here? I only have the one book club so far, but I'm not sure it's a match for you."

"I'm not so much into people. I did my time with the social interaction, but I do need to get down to the bookstore. I've been meaning to find a new book. I enjoy a good mystery now and then." He nodded and then stepped toward the stairs. "I'll be going now. Just glad everything's all right."

"Thanks, Terrance." As Rarity closed the door, she wondered if she'd been wrong. Maybe her mystery-reading neighbor was just the one to join their sleuthing club. Even if he hadn't had cancer. She'd bring it up on Tuesday. They already had a woman actively going through the treatment, and they'd added Sam who hadn't had cancer at all. Maybe there was room for a lonely older man who was looking for a community? She went back to her calendar and made a note on Tuesday's entry page.

Today she needed to research the oncologist whom the scheduling person had set her up with. It was probably fine, but sometimes you could get a feel for someone from their profile. And if this was someone Rarity was going to work with to plan her ongoing health and survival plans, she wanted to know more about the doctor than just her name.

It was almost ten by the time she finished her research. She felt good about this new doctor. Not too young, not too old. She'd been working with the cancer center for a few years. And Rarity had Google-mapped the address to the place next Monday. She'd have her mammogram, then meet with this doctor. And as a treat, she'd take herself to lunch somewhere nice in Flagstaff.

She put everything into her phone calendar so she wouldn't forget, then glanced at Killer. "We've got some time before lunch. Do you think it's too hot for a walk?"

Killer glanced at the window, then snuggled back into his bed.

Rarity laughed at the little dog. "Apparently you're smarter about life in Sedona than I am. Looking at the temperature, you're right that it's too hot. Maybe I'll just take a swim instead."

She started to get up, then noticed an ad for the spa on the same page as the search results for the cancer centers. She sat back down and clicked on the ad. Did people really think they could get rid of something like breast cancer with a few breathing techniques? She knew lowering stress levels could help, but she believed those modalities were best used in combination with modern medicine and treatments.

She shook her head as she read the ad copy. The spa never used the words *cured* or *treatment*. It was lighter than that. More hopeful. And it preyed on the fear surrounding the disease. She flipped through the pictures of the staff again and saw a link to community events.

The spa's doctor was very busy with fund-raisers and cancer events. She flipped through several photos and stopped. Dr. Conrad and his wife could be seen at a table, talking. The couple hadn't noticed the photographer taking a picture of a celebrity, talking to the press in front of them.

Rarity tried to blow up the picture to see the woman who was talking to the doctor. It was Kim. She was married to Dr. Conrad, according to the note below the picture. Maybe it was an error. Maybe the person who had captured the photo had been wrong.

Rarity keyed in *Kimberly Conrad, Arizona*, into the search line. A lot of hits came up, but when she changed it to images, she saw their Kim in several with her "husband," Dr. David Conrad. There was no doubt. Kim was married to the doctor who owned the spa. She didn't just work there. Which explained why she'd been so quick to excuse his actions. Had she only joined the group to get more clients for her husband's clinic?

She tried to call Sam, but no answer. So, she texted her. *DO YOU HAVE TIME FOR LUNCH? WE NEED TO TALK.*

This time Rarity got a quick answer. *NOON AT THE GARNET. I NEED TO CLOSE UP ANYWAY FOR A FEW MINUTES. THIS MORNING HAS BEEN CRAZY.*

Rarity still had time for that swim she'd promised herself. She went to change and work out some of the questions she had as she swam her laps.

When she got to the Garnet, she saw Sam had beaten her there. She slipped into the other side of the booth and opened her menu. "What's your favorite here?"

"Everything." Sam sipped her iced tea. "So, why are you here on a Monday? I thought you were taking those as 'me days' until business picked up."

Rarity gave her order to the waitress who'd stopped by and dropped off a glass of water. Then she answered Sam's question with another question. "What's your take on Kim?"

"What do you mean? She's a little flighty. She hasn't been to a meeting for a couple of weeks. And when she's there, it feels like she's somewhere else. Like she's observing the group and not participating. But that could just be my interpretation. Especially since I don't fit the criteria for the group."

"Neither does she. Or at least, I don't believe so anymore." Rarity nodded to the waitress, who'd dropped off the tea she'd ordered. She wondered if she should have ordered a glass of wine or a beer instead. The swim hadn't calmed her; instead it had brought up new questions about Kim.

"Shirley told you that Kim's just going through treatment. Maybe that's what's bothering you." Sam sipped her tea.

Rarity leaned forward. "I don't think she has cancer at all. I think she's there to get clients for her husband's spa."

Sam didn't say anything as the waitress dropped off their sandwiches. After she'd left, she pointed a fry at Rarity. "That's some serious thinking. Do we have any evidence? The meeting's tomorrow, and if she's there, we can't just out her and not expect fallout. Shirley adores Kim."

"I know. And Shirley's the one I'm worried about. She's dying for companionship. I think her husband is stuck in reliving World War II or maybe the first world war. I can't tell since his book orders cover both wars. But I can tell he doesn't talk to her a lot." Rarity picked up her French Dip and dunked it in the au jus. "And if I'm wrong, Shirley will have to take sides. And we'll lose her."

"The stakes are high on this one," Sam agreed as she bit into her southwestern chicken avocado on wheat.

Rarity focused on her food, twirling the idea around in her mind. Finally, she set the sandwich down and met Sam's gaze. "Especially if Kim killed Martha to keep her from exposing the spa as a fraud."

Chapter 22

Rarity was nervous on Tuesday morning. She was leaving Killer at home with his favorite toys and a potty pad near the door today. She'd made an emergency dog door, but Rarity had found the dog didn't like using it. Especially during the day. At night, she closed it, trying to keep other animals out of the house. Today, she left it closed as well. At least she wouldn't have to worry about Killer. Just the mess he might make in her house. It was worth the peace of mind.

She gave him a hug when she left the house. "Sorry, little dude. I need to know you're here safe and not underfoot if something goes bad at the book club. I know, that sounds silly, but sometimes humans aren't the most rational creatures. And I don't want you to think you need to avenge your Martha's death."

He ran to his bed when she let him down. He'd gotten the message and was sending one of his own. He wasn't happy about being left home.

Rarity waved at Terrance, who was out on his porch watching as she walked past his house to her bookshop. He waved back but didn't try to chat. He must not be a morning person. Rarity had known people like that, but she didn't understand them. Mornings were the best. She got so much work done in the cool of the morning, no matter what her daily to-do list had on it. She unlocked her door and turned over the *Open* sign. Then she got busy.

Before the meeting, she checked the store for visitors, then went over to see Madame Zelda. She had hopefully timed her visit to be between the fortune teller's on-the-hour forty-minute readings.

Madame Zelda looked up from her computer screen as Rarity's entrance was announced by the bells hanging on the door inside her shop. "What do you want now?"

Rarity swallowed and moved toward the counter. "I wanted to ask you a question. I found some spa products in the alley a few nights ago. They were addressed to you."

"So? Is that a crime?" Madame Zelda dropped her gaze back to the computer. "The cops already dropped them off and asked me questions. So no harm, no foul."

"Yes, but I was wondering… Was Martha going to go after the spa for bad treatment? Or false promises? I'm not sure what the legal wording would be."

"Fraud."

A chill went down Rarity's spine. "Fraud?"

"That was what she claimed they did to her. She asked me to go and pretend I was a cancer survivor. The spa gave me the same song and dance they gave her. And they sold me all those products. I threw them away after Martha died. It didn't seem worth the trouble. And I wasn't going back there. Not ever. I've had a real doctor check me out, and I'm fine." Madame Zelda shut the laptop. "When I help a person deal with problems, I'm called a charlatan, a fraud, a taker. But use the word 'doctor' in your name, and you can sell people anything."

"I'm truly sorry for your loss." Madame Zelda was hurting from the loss of her friend, even if she wouldn't hear it.

"Martha was determined. That's why I sent her over to your group. I'd hoped that she would talk to one of you and leave me out of the research side of things. I guess she just didn't have as much time as we'd thought to get the job done."

"Have you told Drew all of this?" Rarity checked her watch. She had five minutes before the book club would start. She needed to reopen the store.

"I told him when he brought back that spa stuff. It's like a bad penny. It just keeps coming back time after time. No matter how far away you throw it." She nodded to the door. "Go to your survivors. I have a client coming in soon."

"Stay safe. These people aren't playing." Rarity moved toward the door.

"I know that. I cancelled all my appointments and told them I wasn't ready to deal with my medical issues right now. That I'd be back when I had made up my mind on what I wanted." She smiled. "Hopefully they'll believe me. Martha flat-out told them they were crooks, and she was going to bring them down. Not the most discreet departure for her."

Rarity smiled. "I think I would have liked Martha had I gotten to know her a little better."

Madame Zelda laughed as the door opened behind where Rarity stood. "I think you're right. You two have a lot in common. Conner, you're right on time. Step into my parlor, and I'll see Ms. Cole out."

Rarity saw the young man blush as he hurried toward the reading room. Rarity stepped through the door and saw Shirley waiting at the door to the bookstore. She turned back to see Madame Zelda peering out the doorway at her. "Have a good evening."

Madame Zelda frowned, then reached out for Rarity's hand. She held it for only a few seconds before she dropped it. "Stay safe. You're in danger." Then she slammed the door and Rarity heard the locks click shut.

"I'm not sure I'm the one I have to worry about," Rarity mumbled as she hurried back to her own store.

Shirley stood from the little bench outside the door. "I figured you were out buying something for the book club."

"No, actually, I totally forgot. It's been a crazy week around here. How are you and George?" Rarity unlocked the store and hurried to move the sign over to the main hallway. "I should start some coffee and get lemonade set up, though."

"Anytime you want me to bring treats, just let me know. I could have whipped up a couple dozen cookies for tonight. Maybe I should run home and bake a batch."

"You're not leaving to go bake. We can get along without cookies for one night." Rarity pointed to the fireplace. "Go sit and I'll be right out."

"Okay, if you say so."

Rarity was coming out of the back when she heard Shirley call out, "Rarity? Did Killer get out? I don't see him anywhere."

"I left him at home for tonight. I was worried it would be too late for the little guy by the time we got done." Rarity felt the lie on her lips, but she didn't want to give away anything to whomever might be listening.

And she'd been right. There were others in the store with Shirley. Sam, Holly, and Malia were all gathered around the fireplace. Rarity set the coffeepot down and plugged it in. There was a tray of cupcakes on the table. Apparently Holly had stopped at the store when Shirley mentioned not baking. "Coffee will be ready in about ten minutes. I'll go get the lemonade."

Sam stood and met Rarity's gaze. "I'll do that. You sit and get the group ready for our chat."

Rarity nodded and pulled out the flip chart. "Anyone have anything new to report?"

"I'm afraid Kelly is off our list. I talked to his alibi, a young woman from Flagstaff. She came into the Garnet looking for him to tell him off. They were together all night when Martha went missing. This Kelly dude is a complete jerk, but it doesn't look like he's a killer. She's so mad at him right now, she wouldn't have lied for him to get him out of a parking ticket. He didn't call after they spent the night together." Holly crossed her legs under her. "I know he was our best suspect, but he didn't do it."

Malia raised her hand. "I talked to Madame Zelda's home neighbors, and they said she was at a party that night and brought home one of the older men in the neighborhood. He said she was surprisingly still there in the morning. Then the guy hit on me, asking if I wanted to check him out. It was gross."

Rarity wrote down the information and pressed her lips together to keep from smiling, or worse, laughing at Malia's estimation of the man's prowess. "Anything else?"

"Kim called and said she couldn't come tonight. She had a work event." Shirley didn't look up from the crocheting she was doing. "I don't think she's very committed to the group. But it's voluntary, right? I guess people should be able to come and go based on their priorities."

"Thanks for the update." Rarity wrote down Kim's name, which made Shirley frown, but then she underlined Madame Zelda's name. "So, I went to chat with our town's fortune teller tonight. That's why the door was locked when you got here, Shirley."

Shirley nodded, her concern over Kim's name being listed forgotten. "Did she tell you anything?"

"I found a box of spa supplies in the alley by the trash last week. They were Madame Zelda's. The same ones the police department found in Martha's house. I went to ask her why she had them." Rarity looked around the room, then dropped the bombshell. "She said she went undercover for Martha at the spa. That Martha thought people there were lying to her."

"Like her doctor?" Malia shook her head. "Man, that's cold. You trust what your health professionals tell you. Otherwise, how can you give informed consent?"

"The spa is telling survivors that their cancer came back and that they can be cured with these treatments." Rarity watched the room, waiting for the dots to be connected. But when that didn't happen, she went on. "It looks like Martha found out and was planning to take legal action against the spa."

"I'm surprised she didn't burn it down. I would have been that mad," Holly admitted. "So, we think that was the motivation for why Martha was killed? That she was going to ruin the spa's reputation?"

"Basically. I know it's a long shot, but with Madame Zelda's information, it rings true." Rarity filled her cup with coffee. "And there's something else."

"You think Kim had something to do with this. Since Martha was here the day when Kim came with me." Shirly pointed to the name. "She's just a sick girl. Why would you push this?"

"Mostly because she's married to the guy who runs the spa." Rarity saw the denial unfolding in Shirley's eyes. "Shirley, she lied to us. I think she was just here to try to get business for her husband's clinic. Maybe Martha recognized her."

"And they went to meet. Remember how Kim was the one to push us all exchanging phone numbers?" Holly leaned toward Shirley. "You said that Rarity wanted to protect us and Kim said—well, she disagreed."

"What did she say?" Rarity looked around at the group. Everyone but Sam had their heads dropped.

"Kim said that night that you were just trying to sell books. That's why you didn't want us to share our phone numbers. And that you didn't care about us." Shirley looked up first. "She was wrong. I'm sorry I brought her into the group."

"Shirley, you don't know what you don't know. Sometimes people don't show their true colors at first." Rarity underlined Kim's name again. "Quick poll, who has gotten a phone call from Kim since giving her your phone number?"

"Not Kim, but the spa has called me three times since then. I guess I was assuming I was on some sort of cancer call sheet," Malia said. She stood up and got a cupcake. "I never associated it with me giving my number to Kim."

"I got those calls, too." Holly stood and poured a cup of coffee. "That's just wrong. You shouldn't try to sell stuff to people who are working through issues. We could have been a serious cancer survivors' group. And then what would have happened? Kim and her husband would have made money off us."

Rarity looked around the group members, who were all staring at Holly.

She paused as she walked back to her chair. "Wait, why are you all looking at me like that?"

"A 'serious' cancer group?" Malia shook her head. "Dude, way to dis us."

"I didn't mean that. I meant we've seemed to have gone on to be a survivors' group *and* a sleuthing group. I don't think anyone here is still freaking out about surviving." Holly's eyes widened. "Sorry, are you guys still dealing with it?"

Rarity smiled and sat down again. "Well, not all the time. But I have been lately. I'm doing my annual mammogram this next week, and I have to say, I'm a little freaked out. I'm meeting a new oncologist too. I'd appreciate good thoughts on Monday."

"We'll do a breakdown next week first thing and let you download all the feelings and ideas." Holly glanced around the group. "Does anyone else need to get something off their chest before we go back to trying to figure out who killed Martha?"

They all shook their heads.

"Okay, so we've crossed off Madame Zelda, Kelly O'Reilly, and that leaves the spa as the motive. Do you really think someone would kill her because of money? Or the opportunity to make money?" Rarity glanced around the circle. Every one of them nodded their heads.

As Shirley did, though, she held up a finger. "We don't know that it was Kim who killed Martha. She might have just said something to the wrong person about Martha being here that night. Maybe someone from the spa wanted to keep her quiet. Someone besides Kim. Come on, guys, you know she couldn't do this."

"Do we really know anything about her?" Sam went to get a cupcake. "I didn't know her as well as you guys did, so maybe I'm off here, but something felt wrong when I met her. She didn't seem honest."

"Which she's not," Malia added.

Shirley glanced at the clock and tucked her crochet project into her bag. "Doesn't mean she's a killer. I've got to go. George hates it when I'm late."

"Okay, we'll see you all next week. Maybe we can find time to talk about the book we planned on reading a few weeks ago." Rarity stood and gave Shirley a hug as she walked by. She whispered in her ear, "You're a good friend."

"You have to be a good friend at my age. You don't have a lot of them left." Shirley patted her face. "You'll be fine at the test. And if you're not, you have us."

"Thanks. I appreciate that." Rarity said good-bye to the rest of the group as they made their way outside. She took the sheets off the flip chart holder and balled them up to throw them away. She saw Sam carrying the almost-empty coffee carafe into the break room. "Hey, you don't have to be the one who stays and helps me clean up, you know."

"Yeah, but if I do, I get to snag a couple of extra cupcakes. I asked Holly if she wanted to take them home, and she laughed at me. I guess she didn't want five cupcakes calling her name when she got home from work tomorrow." Sam dumped the coffee. "So, do you really think Kim's involved in this murder thing?"

"Probably not. I do think she joined the group to push us toward their spa and to make money, though. I can't believe anyone would do that. Pretend they had cancer just to get into a group. Maybe I should ask for a medical bill as proof, to screen out the crazies." Rarity went back out to the front to grab the lemonade. A bang sounded nearby, and she looked out the window to see kids setting off fireworks. She muttered to herself as she was carrying the rest of the food and drink back to the break room. "Keep it up, and I'll be the old lady who calls the cops."

"Who are you talking to?"

Rarity sighed as she poured the drink back into a container and put it in the fridge. She was tired and grumpy, that's all. "Nobody, really. I was talking about the kids setting off fireworks out front. I've never liked those things."

"Me neither. Especially the ones that are only there for the noise. I do like the fountains and blossoms. You're going to love the Fourth of July here. The celebration is crazy." Sam divided up the leftover cupcakes. "I put one in the fridge for tomorrow's lunch dessert. And I'll take two because Drew is coming to walk me home. We can eat them over coffee."

"Better make it decaf or you'll never get to sleep." Rarity grabbed the plastic bag that held her cupcakes and started to turn off the lights. "We'd better get out of here, then, and get you to your date."

"He's meeting me at the shop. I need to grab my tote and stuff. I didn't want to bring it all over tonight." Sam hurried to the door. She held it open as Rarity turned back. "So, where are you going now?"

"I forgot to check the lock on the back door. Go on. I'll be fine. Just turn the lock on the doorknob so no one can get in. I'll be right behind you." Rarity didn't wait for an answer, but when she heard the door close, she smiled to herself. She liked Drew and Sam. They made a good couple, if they would get out of each other's way. Sam was too fast to judge, and Drew, he thought things through way too long. She checked the lock, then headed back into the bookstore and ran right into Kim, who was standing by the break-room door. "Kim? What are you doing here? You're a couple hours late for our book club."

"I hear I was the talk of the group." She held up the flip chart paper. "Why is my name listed as one of the suspects in Martha's killing?"

"It wasn't. I wrote down your name because Shirley mentioned you weren't feeling well. Is your treatment going badly?" Rarity stepped around

Kim and took the paper out of her hand. She tossed it back into the trash can. "My first chemo treatments were horrible. I didn't think I would make it through the treatment plan. Anyway, I can walk with you to your car, but I've got to get home to Killer. He's been by himself all day."

"You think you're so smart. You aren't fooling me, missy." Kim grabbed her arm. "I just want to know how you figured out I killed Martha. And who else besides that group of meddlers knows. I want to get my to-do list finished before I start killing. You're just lucky since you had that break-in at your friend Sam's shop the other night. I'm afraid this time, he wasn't so quick to leave the premises."

"You killed Martha." The words felt like ash in Rarity's mouth. Kim had been on her bad side for trying to get the group to use her husband's spa for treatments, but she'd never really thought Kim could be the murderer. She seemed more like a fifties housewife than a serial killer. Yet, Rarity was going to be number two on her murder list. Or at least the second Rarity knew about.

"Yes, I killed Martha. Don't look so shocked. You had to have figured that out by now." Kim pulled a gun out from behind her back. Then she giggled. "Oh my God. You really hadn't figured it out yet, had you? Damn, I guess I lost the element of surprise. So, the rest of the group doesn't know, either."

"Except when I wind up shot in my store, it's going to make them think twice." Rarity narrowed her eyes. Behind Kim, she could see a face at the door. Sam's face. And soon, it was replaced by Drew's face. She just had to keep Kim talking. Help was on the way. "Look, just leave me alone and I won't tell anyone. You can go set up shop somewhere else, and no one will be the wiser."

"Except Conrad doesn't know what I've done for him. And I'm sure he doesn't want to move. His mother lives down the street from you. Did you know that? I popped out and took a walk to deliver my message the other day. No one saw me. No one's ever on that street except you." Kim stepped toward Rarity. She dropped the gun a little. "I did have something to ask you. I know, you'll be dead and all, but do you mind if I take Martha's dog? I've always wanted a Yorkie, and Killer's so cute. I'll be responsible for him losing both of his mamas, so I guess I owe him that much."

The crazy woman was seriously asking for Rarity's blessing to take Killer after she'd shot her. "I'd appreciate that. I've come to love the little guy, and I'd hate to see him hurt." Rarity reached into her pocket.

"What are you doing?" The gun went back up and pointed at Rarity's face.

She pulled out her key ring. "I was going to give you my house key so you could go get Killer. Like I said, he's been locked up all alone, and I'd hate to have him there until someone finds my body."

"That's thoughtful of you." She nodded to the keys. "Go ahead and give me that, then take that notebook and pen and write down what you've been feeding him. That way I don't have to dig through your cupboards."

"Thank you." Rarity turned to the counter and saw Kim drop the gun to her side. Just then, a crash came from the bookstore's door, and Rarity dove behind the counter, hoping Kim wouldn't follow.

"What the—" Kim shrieked, and then Rarity heard something hard dropped on the other side of the counter.

"Rarity? Are you all right?" Drew's voice called out.

She stood up behind the counter and came face-to-face with the Sedona detective. "Drew, she was going to kill me. And she's the one who killed Martha. She told me so."

"Did not." Kim's speech was a little slurred.

Drew leaned down and put cuffs on her, then dragged her to her feet. "I'm wondering what I'll find at your office at the spa? Sounds like you keep souvenirs from your kills. Seriously, Rarity, were you going to just give Killer to this woman?"

"I was killing time until you came to save me." Rarity moved over to the couch and sank into it. "Can you get her out of here? I'm feeling a little nauseated just having her in my shop."

"Your wish." Drew pulled on Kim's arm. "Let's go have a long talk. And don't think it's going to be pleasant. You're making me miss having a cupcake."

Sam came around the couch and pulled Rarity to her feet. "Are you all right? Did she hurt you?"

Before Rarity could answer, Sam pulled her into a bear hug. "I was so afraid. I thought you'd started working again, so I was going to give you grief about not leaving, then I saw the gun she had pulled on you. Drew almost had to restrain me to keep me from breaking down your door."

Rarity sank back into the couch. "Crap, my door. What am I going to do about that tonight?"

"I can help with that." Archer came into the shop and paused at the couch. "I'll need to run back to my place and get some wood. First up, are you sure you're all right?"

"I'm fine. What are you doing here?" She looked up into his blue eyes.

"Drew said he and Sam were making a night of it, so I came to walk you home. I guess I was a little late for the party." He glanced around the room. "Did Killer get out? Don't tell me that woman hurt him."

"No, he's fine. He's at home. I didn't want him here, just in case there was a scene at the book club. Instead, Kim must have waited until Sam and I were in the back, then snuck inside. That must have been the noise I heard that I thought was fireworks." Rarity met Sam's gaze. "I can't believe she's that far gone. She wanted to know who else thought she was a killer so she could get her list set up first. Like I'd ever tell her."

"Well, hopefully Drew will be able to keep her on ice for a while. We need time to figure out how she killed Martha and why." Sam glanced at the flip chart and picked up a marker. "Maybe I should write this stuff down."

A sound came from the doorway and Drew swooped in and grabbed the marker. "Oh no, you don't. I've already had to save one of your book club crew tonight. Give me a week or so before you do any more sleuthing, okay?"

"I thought you were at the station." Sam actually blushed as she turned away from Drew.

"I dropped her off and came back to help secure the bookstore. She's in a cell, steaming." Drew looked around the bookstore. "I can't believe she just snuck in. She sounds a little drunk."

"Maybe she needed some liquid courage." Sam went to stand by where Rarity sat on the couch. "Why don't I walk Rarity home, and you and Archer can secure her store. Then you can come pick me up at her house and take me home."

"Sounds like a great plan." Drew held out his hands. "Let me help you up, Rarity. Go home, take care of Killer, and by the time we get there, maybe we'll have a confession out of Kim. She has to want to talk. I think the fact that her husband refused to even come down to the station tonight to try to bail her out is a nice starting point."

"You should be at the station, not fixing my door." Rarity grabbed her tote. "But I'm too tired to fight. Come on, Sam. Let's go rescue Killer."

Sam stood and followed her out of the bookstore. "I can't believe she just went unhinged like that. Who did she think we'd think of if you disappeared? She didn't know our friendship if she didn't think I'd go ballistic when you vanished. She would have been the first one I blamed."

A small crowd had gathered around the bookstore. Madame Zelda moved from the group to stand in front of them and block the others. "Is it true? It can't be Kim from the spa, is it?"

"I'm afraid it is. She's the one who killed Martha."

The finality of that statement finally hit Rarity, and she hurried away from the group and down the sidewalk. Sam caught up with her. "Maybe Madame Zelda shouldn't be who you confide in?"

"That's a probably true." She pulled her hair out of the ponytail and then reset it. It was way more complicated than that. She watched the cop car leave the parking lot. "Fame. I can't believe Kim did all of this to make her husband successful. And keep her doctor wife life. I didn't even like showing up for a full class in one of those lecture halls when I was in college. Too many people around."

Then a long ago memory hit her. She'd stood against the wall during her psychology class until Kevin had offered her his seat. Then coffee. Then his bed. Tears filled her eyes. She must be tired if she was crying over Kevin.

"What's wrong now?" Sam reached for her arm.

Rarity shrugged her off. "Nothing. I'm exhausted, scared, and done letting Fate mess with my life. I want a swim."

Chapter 23

On Monday morning, Rarity had finished getting her boobs squeezed by the torture machine some man had to have invented. Every time the technician squeezed down the plastic paddles "one last time" and told her to take a deep breath, she had to fight off the pain. And when they were done, the technician handed her a pink thank-you card for coming in with her phone number, her supervisor's name, and the time frame of when she would hear from the department. She tucked the card into her tote and went to change out of the hospital gown and back into her jeans and tank. Pink was not her color.

She'd liked the new oncologist she'd met at least. The woman was personable and had read through Rarity's file before the appointment. Of course, the results of the test would decide whether there would be any additional treatment, but for right now, she was told to go home and enjoy her day. Maybe she'd top dinner off with a stop by an ice cream shop on the way back to Sedona and get a cone to ease her emotions.

Emotional Eaters R Us. Another book club she could set up with her experience. But with the survivors' club turning into a sleuthing club, what would an emotional eaters' group turn into? She didn't even want to imagine. She stepped out into the desert heat and took an involuntary breath. She didn't think she'd ever get used to this high desert heat, but it was better than the muggy hot weather she'd left in St. Louis.

Her car was to the left in the patient parking lot. As she walked toward it, a man walked toward her, holding a bouquet of flowers. As she got closer, she realized it was Archer. She didn't realize this was a hospital too, but he must be here to visit someone. She stepped closer and smiled. "Hey, stranger. Thanks for fixing my door. The locksmith was there first thing

Wednesday morning and said you'd just left. You need to let me pay you
for the new doors. They're lovely and probably not cheap."

He laughed and nodded. "Not cheap is right. I've got the invoice in my
truck, but if you need some time, I can wait."

"I can buy a couple of doors. I'm not broke—yet." She nodded to the
flowers. "Are you visiting someone?"

He frowned and looked down at the flowers. "No."

"Then why—" The moment she asked the question, she guessed. "Are
these for me?"

"Sam said you were having your first test since beating the cancer, and
I thought maybe you might like some flowers to brighten your day." He
held them out awkwardly. "Unless this is a dumb idea, then yes, I'm here
to visit a long-lost maiden aunt."

She laughed and took the flowers. "I think it's a lovely gesture. But
you could have waited for me to get back to Sedona. You didn't need to
drive all this way."

"If you got bad news, you might have needed a driver." He shrugged.
"And if it was good news, I thought maybe you might want to go on a real
date with me. We can hit a cantina I know for lunch, then go see a movie.
If that works."

"That would be awesome." She leaned into the bouquet to smell the
flowers and take a moment to get her emotions together. "I really appreciate
you coming all this way."

"If I hadn't had a hiking group this morning, I would have offered to
drive you. That way we wouldn't have to drive two cars back to Flagstaff
after our movie." He took her arm and led her to his truck, where he opened
her door. "So, I'm guessing you got good news?"

"Actually, no news is good news. I didn't have to have any additional
scans, which is a good sign. Someone will call me or I'll get a letter in
the next week or so with my results." She climbed into the truck and let
him close the door. She put on her seat belt, then put the flowers on her
lap. She'd have to carry them with her all day if she didn't want them to
get ruined in the heat.

He climbed in, then reached for the flowers. "May I?"

She handed them to him and watched as he opened a cooler in the
backseat, then put the flowers on a towel on top of ice. "As long as we don't
forget them when we get back, they should stay good for a few hours."

"You've thought of everything." She couldn't help comparing Archer
to Kevin, who hadn't even wanted to come to the hospital with her when
she'd had her first surgery. "Thank you for this. It was thoughtful."

He smiled at her and leaned back. "I'm guessing I'm freaking you out just a little here. If this is too much for a first date, I can walk you to your car, and I'll bring the flowers over to you when we're back in Sedona."

"This isn't too much." Rarity swallowed, trying to keep the emotion out of her next words. "Thoughtful is perfect. And you just made the day something to remember in a good way. Thank you."

"You're very welcome. So, can we go eat? I'm starving." He put the truck in gear and backed out of the parking spot. They chatted for a few minutes as he drove them to the restaurant.

As she was getting out of the truck to go eat, she smiled and thought, *No, today didn't suck at all.*

* * * *

Rarity was stocking her healthy living shelf with new books about scams in medical treatment for cancer that she'd found when she'd researched Kim and her husband's spa. The local paper had done an excellent exposé on the place and the questionable medical treatments. She hadn't found a lot of books on ways to choose a responsible doctor or treatment plan, but the ones she had come across were really good. She'd wished she'd found at least one of them back in the day when she was fighting breast cancer. She wouldn't have felt so lost in the jargon.

The bell over the door rang, and she looked up and saw Drew Anderson come into the shop. He picked up one of the books she'd just shelved. "Looks like you've been busy researching. Dr. Conrad is still arguing that he truly believes his patent-pending system is the best way to treat cancer. The fact that Kim was doctoring the reports from the original tests is her failure, not his."

"So, basically he threw her under the bus."

"And then let out the tires. He's a piece of work, that one." Drew took off his hat and leaned down to pick up Killer. "Hey, boy, how are you?"

"He's being horrible, but I love him anyway. What brings you this way?" She walked back to the counter and pulled out a tray of cookies for the book club that night. "Want a snack?"

"Of course." Drew set Killer down, then grabbed a cookie. "I just wanted to warn you that you may be called into depositions next month. Kim's attorney wants to get your testimony thrown out since Kim was under the influence that night."

"He's saying she was drunk? I don't think so. I would have smelled the alcohol."

"Nope. She likes 'Mama's Little Helpers,' as my dad used to call them. Anyway, he's going to subpoena you. I didn't want it to be a shock." He paused. "And I also wanted to let you know something. Shirley's husband, George. He's not at home. I think she's been telling you all that he is."

"Wait, he left her?" Who would leave Shirley? She was an angel, Rarity thought.

Drew shook his head. "Not voluntarily. Rarity, he's in the nursing home. The one that deals with dementia. She goes to see him every week and brings him one of those World War II books she buys. The nurses put it on his bookshelf, but he hasn't been able to read for years now."

"Oh no, that's horrible. Maybe I should tell her to stop buying the books." She felt the tears building up.

"No, don't do that. It's something she can do. He doesn't know, and they have plenty of money. He was an inventor and made a killing off a few processes he developed for mining silver. She needs to think he might come back someday." He shifted on his feet. "Most everyone here in Sedona knows, but I just didn't want you to find out and blow up her fantasy. She's not hurting anyone with what she's doing."

She took a cookie and broke it in half, then ate one side. She pointed the rest of the cookie at him. "You're a good man, Drew. I'm glad you're dating my friend."

He took another cookie, then put on his hat. "Honestly, I'm glad I met Sam. She challenges me. And the best news? Next month, Mom and Dad are moving to Tucson. I'll miss them, but I can travel to see them anytime I want to. And I get my house back."

"Life is coming up roses around here," Rarity called after him.

He turned and nodded. "That's what Archer says, too."

Recipe

I had a Shirley in my life. Not when I was going through cancer, but when I was a young mother in my first professional job and in a horrible marriage. Shirley helped me navigate my feelings and expectations. I hope everyone has a friend in their life who's a little older and a lot wiser. It makes learning how to be an adult so much easier. Anyway, Shirley was an amazing cook, and we held a lot of potlucks at Region IV. Her desserts were always a hit. Sometimes she'd bring in something just because she'd wanted to bake the night before.

Fair warning, this cake has a lot of butter.

Shirley's Texas Sheet Cake
Preheat oven to 350 degrees F and grease a 18x13" pan.
In a heavy saucepan, over medium heat, mix the following:
- 1 cup water
- 1 cup butter (2 sticks)
- 3 Tbsp unsweetened cocoa powder (I love the Hershey's brand.)

In a separate bowl, mix
- 2 cups flour
- 2 cups granulated sugar
- 1 tsp baking soda
- 1/2 tsp salt

In a small bowl, beat together
- 1/2 cup sour cream
- 2 large eggs
- 1 tsp vanilla extract

Mix the wet ingredients with the dry ingredients. After the chocolate mixture boils, remove the pan from the heat and pour it into the batter with the other ingredients. Mix. Pour into greased pan and bake for 15-20 minutes.

While that's baking, make the frosting. In a saucepan, add the following and bring to a boil.

- 6 Tbsps milk
- 3 Tbsps unsweetened cocoa powder
- 1/2 cup butter (1 stick)

After it boils, remove pan from heat and mix in
- 3 3/4 cups powdered sugar

Pour the hot icing over the hot cake and spread evenly with a spatula. Allow cake to set for 10 minutes.

ABOUT THE AUTHOR

Angela Brewer Armstrong at Todd Studios

New York Times and *USA Today* bestselling author **Lynn Cahoon** is an Idaho expat. She grew up living the small-town life she now loves to write about. Currently, she's living with her husband and two fur babies in a small historic town on the banks of the Mississippi River where her imagination tends to wander. Visit her at www.lynncahoon.com.

Printed in the United States
by Baker & Taylor Publisher Services